OUTCAST

Noguchi slowly got to her feet and went to retrieve her burner, not looking at anyone, knowing that those not busy with the queen were watching. Watching and judging, and she didn't need to see the gleeful, derisive stares or the raised mandible; she already knew what that looked like.

They would have lost her. If I hadn't acted, they would have lost her and more would have died.

It didn't matter. She'd branded herself an outsider yet again. It was ridiculous, it was a way of thinking that made no sense—

—and it is the Hunter's way.

Noguchi put up her burner and waited for instruction, humiliated and furious, reminded yet again how very different she was from them—and that no matter how hard she tried, the Hunter's way seemed always beyond her reach.

They didn't like her—and she found out just how very much they wanted her gone when they got the queen back to the ship.

Don't miss any of these exciting *Aliens, Predator,* and *Aliens vs. Predator* adventures from Bantam Books!

PREDATOR™

ALIENS VS. PREDATOR: WAR

S. D. Perry

Based on the Twentieth Century Fox motion pictures,
the designs of H. R. Giger, and the Dark Horse graphic
novel Aliens/Predator: War by Randy Stradley

BANTAM BOOKS
NEW YORK   TORONTO   LONDON   SYDNEY   AUCKLAND

Aliens vs. Predator: War
A Bantam Spectra Book / December 1999

SPECTRA and the portrayal of a boxed "s" are trademarks of
Bantam Books, a division of Random House, Inc.

ISBN 0-553-57732-8

Published simultaneously in the United States and Canada

Bantam Books are published by Bantam Books, a division of Random
House, Inc. Its trademark, consisting of the words "Bantam Books"
and the portrayal of a rooster, is Registered in U.S. Patent and Trademark Office and in other countries. Marca Registrada. Bantam Books,
1540 Broadway, New York, New York 10036.

PRINTED IN THE UNITED STATES OF AMERICA

OPM   10 9 8 7 6 5

For the incredible Zach,
when he's older.

And for Anne Groell, Juliet Combes,
and Lynn Adair—
three women who kick ass on *this* planet.

There is no such thing as an inevitable war.
If war comes it will be from failure
of human wisdom.

—ANDREW B. LAW

ALIENS VS. PREDATOR: WAR

1

They set down just after dawn, or whatever passed for it on the unnamed planet; the dirty light from two distant stars lay across the rocky world like smog, an early bath of murky yellow haze that did nothing to improve Noguchi's mood. It looked like gaseous piss, and even with the steady pump of adrenaline coursing through her, the intensity that came from knowing she was about to face death, she found herself wondering if it was worth it anymore.

In the back. Again. After so many training Hunts that I could teach them myself . . .

They waited for the signal in the main loading dock, the planet's ugly surface displayed on a small screen set into the door. Flashes of glistening black darted across the screen, raising the level of greedy anticipation in the stuffy, overwarm air. Noguchi tried to breathe evenly, wishing that the masks had a better filter system; it was hot, dark, and she couldn't get away from Hunter musk. *Dia-shui*, they called it, along with a clicking that she couldn't pronounce. It was a cloying, animal smell, and the heat made her feel like she was bathing in it.

Probably not so hot up front. Where I belong.

It wasn't a new thought, but it still stung. Noguchi shook herself mentally, working to slide into the focus she would need, to concentrate her energy—but it wouldn't come. She felt overheated and irritated, crowded by the towering young males all around her. The suits had individual thermostats, but even at the low end they were well over human comfort levels, and since the unnamed planet was cold by Hunter standards, the others had theirs cranked up. The heat from their suits combined with the thick, oily musk they secreted, created a humid, feral atmosphere alive with the clicking growls of barely checked excitement. At one time, the sounds and smells had excited her, too, but today it only made her wonder again if this was where she wanted to be.

Focus, focus, focus . . .

Right. It didn't matter that she was in the back, or in the *middle* of the back, the worst position from which to score a kill. Didn't matter that she bore Broken Tusk's mark and was *still* Hunting from the least honorable position—

—stop it! Focus or die, you can't have both.

Beneath the sweaty face mask, Noguchi gritted her teeth, silently cursing her wounded pride. It wasn't the time or place to be bemoaning her lot or letting her emotions take over; this was a queen Hunt. It wouldn't be scored, not burner only, but that didn't mean it was going to be a walk. She kept her gaze front and center, finding Topknot's raised claw and fixing on it. She couldn't see the Leader from her position—most yautja stood two and a half meters, some taller—but the taloned fingers were visible to everyone in the pyramid formation. There were five half-trained novices in a line in front of her, three on either side; the three lead positions were for the more experienced Hunters—

—where I should be—

—and though the Leader was almost always in front, one of the two males behind Topknot had been unBlooded on her first Hunt; even then, she'd outranked him, and on the last Hunt, she'd killed six drones, only one behind Topknot himself—but being *ooman*, as they called it, meant that she'd pulled rear guard. Again.

At least you're here; he could have denied you even this. There are twentysomething trainees just hissing to take your spot. Better to place low than not to place at all—

There was a shuddering rumble all around, the metallic floor shaking underfoot and a flash of brilliant light on the small viewscreen as the ship's weapons laid down cover. Topknot chittered a command and the other yautja raised their burners, growling excitedly, jostling each other in anticipation. Topknot signed as he spoke, one of the simple gestures that was specific to Hunting. "Prepare" was the gist of it, the raised claw twisting back and forth, the talons curled into a fist.

Noguchi held her own burner high, the dark metal of the alien rifle hot and heavy in her hands, feeling her heart start to beat faster. A glance at the screen showed an increase in lithe movement as another rumble shook the ship, as beams of burning light from the carrier shot into the early-morning haze and black bodies flew.

Topknot let out a battle cry, a guttural shriek of bloodlust that pierced the wet heat and brought the others to a frenzy point. More screeching cries and violent hisses filled the shadowy dock, the musk smell growing thicker as the Hunters screamed, shaking back their ropelike locks, holding their weapons high. The passion, the *hunger* was impossible to ignore and Noguchi let it in, her own howling voice lost in the furor, joyously reminded of the reasons she'd joined with them in the first place. She wasn't yautja and maybe they hated her for it, but she shared this one thing with them, this religion of spirit that defined her deepest self.

The Hunt. The kill.

Still screaming, Topknot opened the door and they plunged out into the hazy morning light, a thousand dark drones running to meet them and howling their own warrior cries, teeth dripping and arms grasping. Noguchi picked her first target and fired, feeling nothing but alive.

The queen had called all of her minions home, and though the ship was less than a hundred meters from the hive, they had to fight for every centimeter. Even from her guarded position, Noguchi took out five within the first minute, and the unBlooded were killing beyond their wildest expectations. Even though it wasn't to be officially scored, there was some small honor in numbers.

The hive was in a marshy area and the splashes of the spiny, taloned bugs as they came was a pounding storm, tails whipping up muck, shining exoskeletons mottled with black mud. They didn't come in waves but in a wave; there was no lull in the onslaught, no time to breathe between kills. It was a tsunami of needle teeth and razor claws, of grinning, trumpeting death.

Noguchi didn't think. She danced, swirling and feinting, spinning and firing explosive heat through the wall of bodies. Behind to the left, a shrieking, elongated skull blown into shards. Claws and arms flying in multiple directions, legs smashed and falling, grinning metal teeth shattering. An alien chest bursting with a splash of green acid, the blood hitting the murky water, the swamp turning to bubbling steam before the Hunters had gone a third of the distance.

The fire from the ship continued to clear a path through the worst of it, but there was still no break in the running bodies. Like ants or bees, the drones sacrificed themselves to protect their queen mother, an individual's life meaningless to the good of the hive. They came from everywhere at her beckoning, alerted by some pheromone or telepathy; not even the Hunters knew.

The scents of slime and musk, of fire and some dark and unnatural thing, of *alien* filled the hot, close space inside Noguchi's mask. She didn't smell it, didn't feel the steaming heat, didn't see anything but the next target. And the next. And the next, as the small band of Hunters pushed on to the nest, leaving broken, bleeding creatures in their wake.

As the wall of animals began to thin, Noguchi didn't notice; she was too intent on the blast of blue-white heat coming from the end of her burner, the crash of imploding light that tore into each hard alien body and left it dying or dead. Topknot had stopped at the mouth of the huge, high, rounded shell made of sleek and dusky alien secretion, the queen's egg-laying chamber and home. The drones wouldn't risk damaging the eggs; they were still coming, but the recklessness of their attack had dropped. However they communicated with their queen, they knew to be careful the closer they came to the nest.

Another bug, down, another screaming, clutching monster rushing at her—

—and she was roughly shoved aside.

"Hey! Dammit—"

Noguchi stumbled, hard, her concentration blown for the half second it took her to realize what had happened. She reflexively brought her burner up, pointed it at her assailant, but didn't fire.

Fucking bastard—

The competition for kills on the Hunt was fierce, but there had been no call for what the yautja had done. Except for a very few, the drones had broken off their attack; it gave her ample time to hate him as he took out the drone in her stead. Shorty. Of all the novices, he was the one most often singled out as a target by the others; he was barely a head taller than she, distinctly undersized, and in the weeks that his group had trained under Topknot, he'd gone out of his way to take out his frustrations on her.

"*Ell-osde' pauk!*" Noguchi snarled at him, the yautja equivalent of "fuck you." She'd heard it often enough.

Shorty let out a stream of derisive language. She caught only part of it, *pyode amedha*, "soft meat," a slur for human, and a negative yautja sound for female. She wasn't particularly insulted until she heard her own words echoed back at her.

"*—lei-k'* hey, dammit, *ka'tun-de*!"

He laughed, then, an imitation of human laughter, a braying mockery. Yautja didn't laugh like that; like the mimicry, it was meant to offend.

There wasn't time to dwell on it. Topknot had already stepped into the gaping black mouth of the hive and one of the other Blooded was motioning the trainees inside, covering, only a few dozen bugs still attempting to get close to them. Noguchi shoved past the laughing Hunter, forcing her anger aside as the thick stench of rotting animal flesh washed over her from the darkness. Nests were dangerous, and being pissed at Shorty would take up too much of her awareness.

Doesn't matter. Let him laugh. He didn't know how much better at the Hunt she was than he, and with any luck, she'd soon find opportunity to demonstrate—

—and even as she thought it, she saw a glistening string of liquid drip down from above, a long and sticky drop that spooled past her, almost invisible in the thick shadows. Topknot and most of the others were several meters in front of her, edging into deeper shadow—

—and as she leapt to one side, raising her burner, the drone dropped from above, landing in a crouch only a few meters away, but not facing her. It was silent and quick, its body blending into the dusky light, and Shorty didn't see it until it reached for him.

Noguchi allowed herself a second of total satisfaction as the drone snatched at Shorty's arm, its claws landing heavily on his burner, blocking him from defense. An experienced Hunter might still have a chance, there were the wrist blades, but Shorty was basically fucked.

What goes around . . .

She was in position, but she waited a beat longer until she was absolutely sure that he understood how badly he'd screwed up. She wished she had more time to savor it, but the revenge, however sweet, was still secondary to survival inside the hive. She took a deep breath, and then she did the worst thing she could possibly do to Shorty.

The blast from her weapon caught the bug in its abdomen, its snaking green guts blown off into the dark. Even with the alien screams from outside, Noguchi could hear the gangly body clatter to the floor, and the silent appraisal from the Hunters behind her was a palatable thing. No way they'd missed what had happened.

The mask hid her grin, and there was no point in laughing. If there was any greater dishonor in Clan etiquette, she'd never heard of it. Not only had he been denied an honorable death, his peers and betters had just seen him have his fighting done for him—and by an alien, no less, one even smaller than he.

Shorty stood perfectly still, head tilted down at the drone body. One of the other young males started to laugh, a clattering, trilling sound that always made her think of a bird with a broken windpipe trying to sing. He was quickly joined by the others.

Not so much fun being laughed at, is it?

Noguchi shot a look at the assembled Hunters in time to see Topknot signal ''enough'' and growl a command to Shorty. She only recognized the sound of his name, but knew what Topknot had asked even before Shorty walked stiffly toward the Leader; he'd been assigned to be in the middle of the hive line, protected front and back.

He wouldn't laugh at her anymore, but it would be wisest not to let her guard down until Shorty was Blooded and gone. She almost felt bad for him, but reminded herself that if he wasn't such an asshole, she would have let him die; he deserved the dishonor, for being such a goddamn bully.

Topknot signaled for them to proceed, Noguchi taking her position second to last—Shorty's place. When someone screwed up in battle, the other yautja generally congratulated each other on getting a better spot, a growling, shoving version of a high five—but no one would look at her, and as they started down the entry tunnel, the temperature and humidity rising with each uneven step, Noguchi felt as isolated and ignored as usual.

Doesn't matter, I don't need their approval to Hunt and if I wanted friends, I would have left Ryushi with the colonists, gone back to Earth.

Where she'd never had any friends.

Before they'd gone ten meters, all of her defenses were securely back in place. The queen was close, and the thrill of knowing she'd be facing a queen mother again, even as part of a team, would go a long way to compensate for the loneliness of the past year. The drones were as stupid and mindless as ants, but the egg-layer, the queen . . .

An opponent worthy of respect, cunning and resourceful—and one she felt more of a connection to than any of the yautja she'd encountered, with the exception of the one they'd called Dachande, Broken Tusk. The one who'd died after Blooding her, after the massacre on Ryushi. The one who'd led her to believe that the yautja were a race capable of appreciating any skilled Hunter, no matter what species—

Behind her, Scar clattered an angry warning for her to move faster and kicked at the back of her leg. It would have hurt if she hadn't stepped quickly forward at the sound of his voice. As unpopular as Shorty was, he was yautja—and even after such a monumental fuckup, he was still more popular than she.

So much for appreciation. Noguchi clenched her jaw and reminded herself that the queen was close.

2

Ellis was strapped in and asleep, and Jess obviously wasn't in the mood to talk; he stared sullenly at the vidscreen from the copilot seat, at the passing black of space as he'd done for the last four hours. Not a word, and although Lara wouldn't have minded a little conversation, she didn't want to invade his privacy. Privacy on the small shuttle meant closing your eyes when someone needed to pee, a difficult enough activity in zero grav; if Jess wanted to be alone with his thoughts, she could at least give him that.

Not much point in making small talk anyway . . .

Lara closed her tired, grainy eyes for a moment, amazed that the thought of their upcoming deaths hadn't lost any of its punch. They'd lived with it for almost three days, and it still made her stomach knot each time she thought of it, even after the nightmare of 949. She'd been prepared, then, with other lives depending on her actions. Now, though . . . she didn't want to die, and she particularly didn't want to die from asphyxiation in a cramped, cold shuttle in the depths of space. Even with the patch job on the filters, they only had another fifteen, twenty hours of breathe time. And though DS 949 hadn't been as DS as most, the shuttle's bare-bones navigation system was strictly self-contained, no hookups, not even a list of planets or 'toids in the quadrant; it had been designed as a go-between, ship to shore, not for deep-space transport—which meant, simply, that if there was anywhere to go, they weren't going to find it.

She opened her eyes, looking again at the trail of glowing green numbers on the small console screen. They'd been headed .82 since bailing from the terminal, only because she thought she remembered a survey office somewhere in the low eights; it was a long shot, but it wasn't like they had any alternatives. If they were on the *Nemesis*, they'd have been picked up by now; their old ship had been wired for serious range—

—and it was blown to shit along with Pop, the station, and about a million alien bugs. Why not wish for something you can have, like freeze-dried bean curd? Or a nap?

Sleep sounded good. She'd caught a few hours earlier, but it had been more like falling unconscious than real sleep. Ellis had been knocked out for most of their trip, which was just as well; the Max interface had done a number on him, and not just physically. The kid had saved their lives, for what it was worth, but it had cost him.

Lara glanced at Jess and tried to remember the last time he'd slept. Just after the escape, she thought. The loss of Teape and Candyman had been bad for him, worse than for her or Ellis; both men had died badly, and under his command. She'd tried telling him that it was Pop's fault, Pop and the Company's greedy indifference to the Max teams, but Jess seemed determined to take it on himself.

Sixty hours? More?

"Jess, you wanna catch a few zees? I'll stay up, make sure the beacon doesn't conk out . . ."

Jess started as if from a trance. He looked over at

her, his face expressionless. ''No, that's okay. I'm good.''

Lara studied him, his deep brown features set into grim lines, the exhaustion and hurt and shame in his gaze. Tired and sad she could live with, but she'd left him alone about what had happened for long enough; too long, maybe.

''Martin, it wasn't you,'' she said softly, and saw him wince ever so slightly, a tightening around his mouth and eyes. ''And you know it. Why are you doing this?''

Jess looked away, staring down at the backs of his hands. ''I don't want to talk about this—''

Lara shook her head, feeling a sudden rush of anger at him, at his stupid male need to keep it all for himself. ''Well, that's too bad, Jess. What if it was all my fault? If I'd told you about how weird Pop was acting, maybe we could have stopped him. Or Ellis, why don't you put it on him? If he'd gotten into Max a few minutes earlier, they might still be alive. Why you, why do you want to take responsibility for this?''

For a moment he didn't answer, his jaw clenched, his mouth a thin line. The low hum of the 'cyclers was all there was to hear, pushing barely warmed air through the dying filters. Lara wondered if she'd gone too far; she'd been contracted, ex-Marine, while Jess and his two men had been fighting XTs in lieu of prison time. There was always a distance between the ''volunteers'' and the Company staff—

—and to hell with it. We're going to die together, to hell with going too far. It doesn't matter anymore. If it ever did.

Jess finally looked up at her, and because she expected him to be defensive and angry, she was a little surprised by the open sorrow she saw across his weary features.

''Because no one else will,'' he said. ''Pop's dead, and Weyland/Yutani had us sacrificed before we even got the call. There's—there's no one else to feel shitty about what happened. To be responsible.''

He sighed again, looking away. "They deserve that," he said, so quietly that she didn't think he'd meant it for her.

His reasoning was terrible, but she could see the rough logic in it; for a man who hadn't slept in three days it probably made perfect sense. Ellis wasn't the only one damaged by what had happened.

"Tell you what," she said gently. "You sleep, and I'll think about Teape and Pulaski for a while."

Jess blinked. "Don't patronize me, Lara—"

She shook her head. "No, really. You're right, everyone thought they were expendable. The Company wanted us dead for finding out that the infestation came in on one of their ships; no witnesses, Pop said. And whatever data they wanted off that log, it meant more to them than any of us. Teape and the Candyman were good guys, and they deserved better than what they got. It's still not your fault, but I understand what you're saying."

Lara took a deep breath and met his gaze evenly. "Go rest. I'll stay up and watch things . . . and I'll carry it for a while. Okay?"

It was Jess's turn to study her, and he must have seen that she meant it because after a moment he nodded slowly. "Okay," he said. "Just a few minutes."

He unstrapped himself and floated past her chair, headed to one of the wall slings at the rear, next to where Ellis slept and the Max sat, cold and empty and dead. Lara leaned back, closing her eyes, feeling useless. Jess would get some sleep anyway, that was good.

Wouldn't want to meet oblivion with bags under your eyes. Lord knows you want to be well rested, sharp, and alert so that you can panic fully when you start to lose consciousness . . .

She told herself to shut up and thought about Teape and Candyman Pulaski, about how they'd died. It wasn't much of a favor to Jess; she'd thought of little else since they'd left the terminal. She'd thought of Ellis, climbing into the suit to save Jess in spite of the interface that had fucked him up so thoroughly. Of the poor bastard who'd been inside the Max first, who'd died alone and insane in the metal shell because the Company had put him there. Of Eric "Pop" Izzard, her lover who had made a deal and screwed all of them, and of the four hundred people of DS 949 who were no more because somebody had fucked up on quarantine.

All of that, and how they were going to die soon.

Lara opened her eyes and started looking through the scant computer files on quadrant layout for the hundredth time; she had nothing better to do.

Ellis woke up with the same headache he'd had for years, or what seemed like years. For just a moment, he didn't know where he was or why he was surrounded by clingy web, by lines of dusty thread that lay across his skin like a cold whisper—and then he saw the dented orange metal of Max's massive right arm some three meters away, the blackened metal of its flamethrower "hand" reflecting the bare light beneath the securing straps, and closed his eyes again.

Safe, I'm safe. My name is Brian Ellis. Brian Ellis, I'm twenty-four, A-level in synth repair and contracted to Weyland/Yutani and I'm in the shuttle from, from—

For a second, he could only see images. A plain bunk. A cramped room with thick plexi windows and the giant steel table where Max slept. A stats/med console, blue lines pulsing across. He saw Pop's angry face and then a dead and rotting body, its face grinning, a decaying, stinking man on the floor of 949, just after he'd brought Max over from—

"Nemesis," he whispered, and felt a rush of relief. Compared to before, the name had come easily. As he'd done each time he'd awakened on the shuttle, he brought himself up-to-date, checking for lapses. The first time he'd opened his eyes after the station, all he'd known was Lara's name and his own age.

He, they, were on the shuttle from the *Nemesis.* He'd been part of a Max team, assigned to monitor the

machine's human occupant and run its program in order to clear XT infestations—

—33, first 011.2 away—

—and they'd gone to deep-space terminal 949, and
he'd gone into Max himself when everything had gone
wrong. When Pop had deserted the team and the man
in Max had died, his wasted body pushed too far by the
synth adrenaline. Max's interface had been designed to
fit into a surgical implant, which Ellis didn't have; the
prongs had pierced his skull, and he and Max had become one, one perfect machine that dealt death from
both hands, wiping the bugs—

*—space 17.25 object dot nine the animals cooking in
their shells acid boiling my name is Brian—*

Ellis blinked, forcing himself to think clearly. The
station had been fail-safed and Lara had picked them
up in the shuttle. In *this* shuttle, he and Jess, and the
interface had *not* been perfect. It had done damage,
possibly long-term—but then, he'd probably never
know.

He heard a soft grunt from the mesh bunk below
and looked down to see that Jess was asleep. Even in
rest, his features were strained, his hands in fists; he
was sad and angry, grieving over the Candyman and
. . . and the man with the thin, twitchy face and
haunted eyes. The bait. The volunteer who found the
egg chamber by letting himself be caught . . .

Teape. Teape, the Candyman had called him "Tee-
pee."

Getting better, and how much time? How long now? He
knew the air filters were going, he'd at least gotten that
much in one of his earlier bouts of consciousness. Once
they wound down, the air would turn to poison in a
few hours. Strangely, the thought wasn't as terrible as
it should have been.

Ellis sat up slowly, pulling the tab on the bunk and
letting himself roll out into the frigid air, careful not to
bump into Jess. The scabbed wound on the back of his
head itched beneath the Plastical patch, but it wasn't

throbbing anymore and he didn't feel like throwing up; a definite improvement. He pulled his glasses out of his front pocket and slipped them on, the tight interior of the shuttle instantly becoming sharper and even smaller than when it was a blur.

Lara was at the ops console in the front, slouched in front of the nav screen. Ellis shifted himself to one side and pulled himself along using the handholds on the wall, waiting until he was well away from Jess before speaking.

"Lara?"

She turned and he saw the exhausted worry in her eyes for just a second before she pasted on a shaky smile, a few tendrils of her long hair swirling around her face.

"Hey, Ellis. How are you feeling?" Her concern, at least, seemed genuine.

"A lot better. I'm—I can remember things pretty clearly now, I think. I've still got a headache, but not as bad."

Lara nodded, her smile a little more real. "That's great, I'm really glad to hear it. Are you hungry? You haven't eaten since like 1400 yesterday. . . ."

Ellis pulled himself closer, grabbing the molded plastic arm of the other chair. "How long was I asleep?"

"Fourteen, fifteen hours. Don't worry, we still got almost a full day left and plenty of power on the signal. Someone could still hear us."

Katherine Lara had been a second lieutenant in the USCMC before having her contract bought up by the Company, and had proved herself to be fast and graceful under extreme pressure—but she couldn't lie for shit. As out of it as he'd been, Ellis had still been able to comprehend that their chances were one in a million.

Lara started digging through one of the packs hanging on the wall as Ellis moved to the chair and sat, loosely strapping himself in.

"Let's see, we got . . . soypro in sweet and sour,

grilled and with onion . . . fish and veggie . . . and there's one lemon chicken left."

Ellis shrugged. "All kinda tastes the same anyway."

"No, the chicken's not so bad, the texture's really close." She handed him the thin pack and Ellis pulled the plastic spork off the side and unzipped the seal. In 9.61 seconds, scented steam rose from the pouch and he realized that he was ravenous; he burned his mouth on the first few bites, not caring at all.

"What'd I tell you," Lara said. "Way better than the beef."

Ellis nodded, swallowing, thinking of how much things had changed for him in only a few days. He'd been a novice tech before DS 949, signing up for the Max team to make up for a lifetime of feeling powerless, of being too skinny, too smart, too socially inept; his own father had ridiculed him for his weaknesses . . .

. . . *and now? I'm dazed and in pain, we're probably going to die, and I don't know that I've ever felt more at peace. I did something, I made the decision, and then we made it happen.*

Being inside of Max had been . . . he, they, had been *important*. Now that his mind was his own again, he would be able to live his final hours with some real dignity. With the awareness that when things had gotten bad, he and Max had acted.

He finished the chicken and turned to see Lara dozing in her seat, her slender neck arching back, strands of reddish hair that had escaped her ponytail forming a gentle halo around her pale face. She was beautiful, he'd thought so since joining the *Nemesis* team, but hadn't thought she could possibly be interested in him . . . still, he had clear memories of her sweet and frowning face in front of his, the sound of her kind, lilting voice reaching into the haze of confusion that had taken up so much of the past—

—*seventy-four hours estimate fourteen minutes variable*—

—few days. Maybe it was only because he'd been sick, or wishful thinking on his part—

—*or maybe she sees me differently now. Because I'm not the same dumb-ass kid I was.*

Ellis leaned back in his chair, thinking that it didn't really matter if she liked him in that way. What mattered was that it was possible, that for the first time in his life he felt like someone, a pretty woman no less, might actually be impressed by him.

First, and maybe last. Ellis watched her sleep, feeling a deep sense of contentment. He'd been a hero, even if only for a little while, the mind inside of a Mobile Assault Exo-Warrior, a giant with hands of fire and death.

It was a dream he could live on, for as long as they had left.

3

*T*he long corridor was tinted red and teeming with alien life, the giant bugs tearing toward them lightning fast—

—and Jess shouted to be heard, his heart in his throat, hearing nothing but alien screams. Something had gone wrong with their transmitters. "Lara, Pop, we're losing you!"

There were a dozen down now, torn to dusky pieces as the three men fired and kept firing. Shrieking drones leapt over their fallen siblings, a relentless charge into the team's curtain of explosive fire.

The Candyman yelled, the words rising clear and strong over the screeching attack. "Line's dead, can't hear you on the 'set!"

It was bad, a bad place to be, and it could only get worse. A bug scrabbled toward him, clawing through the growing pile of dead or dying drones, limbs and bodies melting through the deck in oozing acid-splash. Jess fired, the rifle pushed to full auto, hot and jumping, and the monster's head was suddenly gone.

Even as it collapsed, he could see others behind it, closing the distance and oblivious to their own mortality. Jess shouted again into the static of his mike, hoping against hope, and there was nothing. They were cut off.

Part of the deck had melted through and several of the maimed bodies dropped out of sight, disappearing through the growing, smoking hole, and still they advanced, barely slowed by the awesome hail of armor-piercing rounds. He made the only decision he could, praying that Teape and Pulaski could hear him over the intensifying attack.

"Fall back! Too many, fall back! Sound off!"

Jess fired again, shuffling back a half step, risking a glance at the boys—

—and felt his gut plummet, felt his mind teeter on the brink of something vast and terrible. Both men were firing, holding the line—except Pulaski's abdomen was shredded, slippery coils of intestine hanging down to his knees in purple ropes. He was grinning the wide grin that spoke of his love for the fight, but his teeth were outlined in red, blood dripping from the corners of his mouth.

Past him was Teape, Jess knew it even though he couldn't see his face. Teape wore the flat crab body of a hatchling, its long tail wrapped tightly around his throat, its spidery, muscular legs curving around the back of his skull. Somehow Teape could still see his targets, picking them out from the seemingly endless river of teeth and claws—

—and Jess had stopped firing but the drones weren't reaching him, running and screaming but not getting close enough to take him down.

"Fuckin' hell of a ride, Jess!" Candyman screamed, bloody mist spraying from his red teeth, and Teape didn't, couldn't speak, only turned his head in Jess's direction, the noose of the face-hugger's smooth, scaled tail slipping tighter around his throat.

Pulaski looked at Jess, blasting the oncoming wave without targeting, his eyes filmed cataract-white.

"You better get outta here, Jessie," he said, his voice suddenly a dull, dead monotone but louder than anything else. "We're dead already."

Jess opened his mouth to resist, to tell them that he would

*stay, that he wouldn't leave them—and nothing at all came
out, no matter how hard he struggled. He drew in lungfuls of
air, determined to scream, to be heard over the dying howls
of the drones and the rattle of pulse fire, above the stench of
blood and burning—*

—and woke up.

For a moment, Jess didn't move, staring at the
empty net overhead, afraid to close his eyes again.
Slowly, his heart stopped pounding and the light sheen
of sweat that the nightmare had left on his brow turned
cold. Still, he didn't move, not wanting to; there was
nowhere to go, anyway.

The intense feelings of guilt and horror he'd felt in
his dream faded, leaving him both wrung out and
strangely thoughtful. He closed his eyes again, thinking
about the dream, about the conflicted feelings he'd had
since they'd escaped the station. Horror, sorrow,
guilt—and some dark and heavy feeling that he hadn't
examined too carefully. The horror and sadness were
obvious; the rest of it, he thought it might be worth to
try and work through. He wouldn't have much longer
to make his peace.

Teape and Pulaski, dead. He wasn't suffering survivor's guilt, or at least he didn't think so; he'd made it
because that was how things had worked out, right or
wrong—and considering where he and Lara and the
kid had ended up, "making it" and "survivor" didn't
really seem to apply. He wasn't bothered overmuch
about checking out, although not because he felt he deserved it; the simple truth was, there was no point in
being bothered by what he couldn't change.

*Maybe it's just that I didn't see it coming. As fucked as
the Company is, I still thought that they'd play us fair—and
if I'd been paying attention, maybe I could have done something.*

Worthless thinking; it was already done. Jess
sighed and glanced at his watch; he'd been out for five
and a half hours, enough to be semisane for a while. He

felt tired and low, but better than when he'd sacked out. At least now, he'd be able to think straight.

And is that a good idea? Maybe you should just go back to sleep. Because if you think about what happened . . .

There it was, that deeply uncomfortable feeling that he'd avoided as long as he could. He knew what it was; anger, the kind that overwhelmed intelligence, that blocked out reason. Hatred with no outlet, no place to go but deeper inside. Those men had died because some Company suit had wanted a download from one of the ships docked at 949, the ship that had brought the bugs inside, and the blind fury burning inside of him would stay until he died—or until the Company paid for what it had done. The former was a hell of a lot more likely, and that only fueled the red and melting heat of his frustrated rage.

And that scares the shit out of you, doesn't it? his mind whispered. *Dying angry.*

Yes. He'd grown up angry, and that undirected rage was what had made him a volunteer in the first place; it had led him to murder a couple of lowlifes in a fit of passionate rage, it had led him to prison. He'd never been one to wallow in his past, coming to uneasy terms with what he'd done after a lot of introspection and a shitload of psych vids . . . but the emotion that had put him there . . .

What was so troubling was that he felt that he'd *conquered* it, that he'd learned how to ease himself out of his violent emotions. He could be angry without letting it rule him.

Yeah, right. No problem.

Thinking about what had happened to his team, that serenity he'd worked so hard to attain access to was gone. It was a feeling both familiar and terrible, a feeling that he had no control over his emotions. He was afraid of dying without any sense of calm, that hopeless fury bright and seething in his heart.

The Company. The goddamn Company.

Jess heard Lara and Ellis in the front, talking softly,

and decided that he'd stay where he was, just a moment or two longer. He might not be able to come to terms with the great injustice that had been done to them before their time ran out, but he needed to try. He needed to at least navigate a path through the twisting bonds of his fury, whether or not he could walk it.

It was funny; even a year ago, he would have laughed himself silly over the idea that he'd spend his last hours trying to better himself. He'd gone from being a gun-running banger with little or no self-awareness to a con to an H/K volunteer—and somewhere along the way, he'd figured out what being a man, what being a *human* was really about . . .

Jess shook his head, wondering where his sense of humor had gone. Fuck it. He was going to die, and hating the Company felt good because it deserved to be hated.

That brought a smile to his lips; sometimes, simple was best.

After a time, he drifted back into a light, dreamless doze, thoughts of revenge keeping him warm as the shuttle spun through the endless black.

As they got closer to the egg chamber, the stink of moldy flesh grew, a smell like sickness and rot and the desperation of a slaughterhouse. Noguchi heard the soft hissing of hidden drones, but the only movement in the shadowy, blighted structure was their own. Attack inside of a nest was highly unlikely.

In spite of their size, the Hunters moved with hardly a sound, only a whisper of padded armor brushing against itself and the occasional soft splash of a clawed foot in pooled and fetid water, those noises from the unBlooded. Xenophobic and violent, maybe, but an experienced Hunter had no equal in grace or stealth when he put his mind to it. There were no female yautja Hunters that she knew of, although the males did speak of their counterparts respectfully; in truth, she simply didn't know very much about the intricacies of their culture, even after a year. She'd grown tired of asking after being openly ignored for so long . . .

Her mind was wandering. A defense against the smells and heat, against the memory of what had happened on Ryushi. The alien queen accepted almost any large animal to act as incubator for her young; on Ryushi, it had been rhynth at first, the hatched face-huggers implanting the slow-moving, cattlelike animals, the queen forming a makeshift nest on the transport ship *Lector*. Of course, humans had been next, and she'd met the Leader Dachande in the subsequent nightmare; he'd brought his students to the seeded planet, unaware of the human colony, and the un-Blooded males had decided to Hunt "ooman" after Broken Tusk had been wounded.

There were strict rules against Hunting intelligent species, she knew, but she also knew that there were many yautja who wanted those "laws" repealed; Broken Tusk's students had proved that clearly enough.

Together, she and the injured Leader had taken out the queen and saved most of the colonists, Broken Tusk slaying several of his students for what they had done. His dying act had been to engrave his jagged symbol between her eyes, the sign that she was worthy of Hunt . . .

. . . and you're still trying to distract yourself, to keep your mind busy. Because you know what's coming.

Topknot had already led the majority of the Hunters around a curve ahead, the dark matter secreted by the drones forming extremely hard and somehow light absorbent walls, all of the hive as sleek and organic in appearance as she imagined melted rock would be. From the now nearly overpowering reek, she knew that they had reached the egg chamber. And while Noguchi was impatient to meet the queen, she wasn't looking forward to—

—to this.

Holding her burner at the ready, Noguchi stepped

into the hot and shadowy, stinking lair, absorbing the environment as Topknot directed several of the students to unload their equipment. According to Hunter lore, the bugs had evolved on many worlds simultaneously; it saved them from having to take responsibility for spreading the breed so that they might Hunt. And although she had worked not to concern herself with philosophies that she had no hope of changing, the result of the yautja "seeding" was what was in front of them now. The incubators were different, but in almost every other respect, it was just like the *Lector*.

The ruptured bodies strung to the walls of the *Lector* had primarily been those of rhynth; the creatures here were vaguely humanoid, four long, fleshy pink limbs, heads with two eyes, hands with digits. The slack, open mouths were filled with pointed teeth— open, perhaps, in expressions of pain and terror. The large empty shells in front of them, their fleshy petals peeled open, and the holes in their strange pink chests, burst out from inside, told the rest of the familiar story in simple strokes. Noguchi could see over a dozen of the life-forms from where she stood, hanging randomly from the walls like dead ornaments, and the chamber stretched off into shadows too deep for her to imagine how many more had been implanted. What little light there was came from small, uneven holes in the ceiling high above, filtering down in sickly streaks.

At least these are dead, they're not suffering anymore . . .

A useless rationalization. Wherever the bugs went, the habitat was destroyed, certainly wiping out entire species; all kinds of indigenous life would suffer for untold generations. And on a more immediate level, Noguchi could hear rasping, mewling sounds coming from somewhere across the vast space, soft and droning. The noises were not bug; she could only hope that the living incubators were deeply asleep, perhaps dreaming of life, spared the horror of their fates until the very end.

Topknot signaled and spoke, telling the chosen

eight to ready themselves. They hefted their coils of rope, a heavy, braided leatherlike material that was stronger than anything humans had. Topknot's briefing aboard the ship had been fairly straightforward; the capture team would rope the queen and hold her down while the Leader cut her from her egg sac. The other four Hunters—herself included—would perform the basically unnecessary task of watching for drone attack.

The Leader moved easily into the dark, veering left, the others falling into position behind him. Noguchi covered the right rear flank, her frustration eased only a little by the sight of Shorty covering right front. It was nice that the spotlight wasn't on her for a change. As senior Hunters on the ship, Topknot, Scar, and Three-Spot were used to her, as were the regular crew— mostly Blooded yautja too old to fight anymore. However they felt about it, they didn't study her every move on Hunt. But with each new training group, Noguchi was made painfully aware of how unprecedented her presence was; they watched her as she might once have watched some animal performing tricks. By fucking up, Shorty had taken some of the scrutiny off of her; his peers would be watching to see if he was competent, the unBlooded always eager to improve their caste—

—a low hiss. From the blackness in front of them.

Topknot stopped and raised his claw, the ropers spreading out. Noguchi's heart was hammering and she was barely aware of the sudden smile on her face as she sidled farther right—

—and with a thundering, piercing scream, the queen lunged forward from the dark, her multiple talons reaching out to rip and tear, her grinning, wet jaws snapping for blood.

The yautja fell back, leaping quickly out of reach. As expected, the queen was unwilling to jeopardize her unborn children by abandoning her egg sac, a long diaphanous tube filled with her developing brood. She hissed and shrieked at the Hunters from atop her gelid throne, slick drool sliding from her incisors, her inner jaws lowering into a strike position.

Noguchi gazed up at her in awe, struck by her incredible design, by the mammoth shining comb that swept back from her eyeless, phallic skull. Her four arms snatched and clawed, her entire body trembling with rage. Twice as big as a drone, a thousand times as deadly because she could *think*.

"Dahdtoudi!" Scar growled, and Noguchi shook herself at the sound of her Hunter name, forcing her attention away from the feral queen. She stared off into the empty dark, holding her burner ready, reminding herself that there would be time later; now, she had to fulfill her assigned task. No matter how pointless.

The queen screamed as the Hunters went to work, her seething fury echoing through the stinking dark. And somehow, the sound made Noguchi feel much better about how her life was turning out.

4

Things were fine until Three-Spot lost his focus.

The queen was a force unto herself, a writhing tangle of arms and teeth and fury—but there were eight full-grown yautja holding her down, a Hunter for each limb and two holding her head back, their ropes hooked around the widest section of her dusky comb. Three-Spot, one of Topknot's Blooded, was braced in front of her, his rope wrapped several times around her upper left wrist.

Noguchi stood only a few meters from the struggling yautja, forcing herself to continue her watch and running through what would happen next. Once the queen was subdued—as close to it as they could hope to get—Topknot would pull his *h'sai-de*, a kind of scythe-sword, and slice the thick membrane between her and her egg sac. At once, the Hunters would start pulling her forward, moving to keep their captive off-balance. Those holding her arms would crisscross around her, tying both sets to her ribbed chest. With her head still held back, they'd lead her out of the hive,

the Hunters making certain that the queen was constantly aware of the burners aimed at her; the breed's
reverence for the egg-layer and the queen's own survival instincts would keep the drones at bay. As long as
the Hunters holding the ropes were vigilant, the walk
back to the ship should be uneventful—until it was
time to get her aboard. Topknot had explained that
then was often the most dangerous part. The queen
would know it was her last chance and—

Three-Spot let out a grunting gasp and Noguchi
spun in time to see the Hunter jerked off his feet. The
queen screeched, raising her arm high, swinging the
yautja around easily before slamming him to the floor
of the nest.

In the split second it took for her to assess the situation, Noguchi saw that Topknot had already cut her
loose—and in that same instant, the queen took one
thundering step forward—

—and brought her giant, taloned foot down on
Three-Spot's chest. The splintering *crunch* was audible
even over the mother bug's screams and Topknot's
hissing commands, the heavy bone of the Hunter's
breastplate giving like dry wood.

The capture team was in trouble. Free from her
ovipositor sac and with one arm loose, the queen sidled
to the right, the movement swift and graceful. Four of
the Hunters were knocked to the ground, and although
they still held on to the restraints, the queen's freedom
was imminent. She shook her head from side to side,
screaming, leaning back in order to lunge—

—and Noguchi was moving before she could think
about it, dropping her burner and taking two running,
leaping steps to snatch at Three-Spot's rope.

The queen saw her coming just before Noguchi
grabbed the restraint. The black-clawed foot came up,
dripping with yautja blood—but she was too late. Noguchi's gloved grip was solid and she fell backwards,
becoming deadweight as she pushed her heels into the
ground.

A year with the Clan and Noguchi's strength astounded even her, but her weight was less than half of a grown yautja's. She only had to manage for the few critical seconds that Topknot would need—

—and they had it. The cries of the Hunters told her that they were in control again, as they sounded off their positions to the Leader. Noguchi held on to the rope but didn't look to Topknot, transfixed by the snarling queen. Four meters tall in a crouch. As close as she was, the strangely polished look of her, the incredible mass and raw power, the absence of heat radiating from her like she was drawing life into herself was—

Whack!

The back of Topknot's hand against her shoulder was enough to knock her over and roll her across the dark, stinking floor, another Hunter already at her position.

Noguchi could have turned the fall into a shoulder roll and come up, but she knew from painful experience that she'd be sorry for it. Landing on her back, she immediately moved into a crouch and brought her hands up, palms out as if to ward off a blow, tipping her face down and looking up at Topknot from under her lashes, the mask's shaded eye slits tinting him red. Between hisses, clicks and movement, yautja language was often complicated; this one was easy.

I submit. You are stronger.

Topknot raised his claw as if to hit her again, then pointed at the queen, restrained again by the capture team. He growled out the sound of Three-Spot's name and tilted his head forward. *You were wrong to take Three-Spot's place.*

Noguchi didn't, couldn't respond until he signaled that he was done. Her cheeks burning, she held her submissive pose and waited for him to finish.

Topknot made a fist and tapped his chest, then pointed at her, clattering an angry phrase punctuated by hissing, one of the many sayings that Hunters used to communicate. *I am Leader and your position was as-*

signed, the movements told her. She didn't know the direct translation for the proverb, but the gist of his words was that the failure of one was the failure of all. She'd heard it more than once in the past months; it was one of the Leader's favorite reprimands.

Without another word or sign, Topknot turned away and moved back to command the capture team.

Noguchi slowly got to her feet and went to retrieve her burner, not looking at anyone, knowing that those not busy with the queen were watching. Watching and judging, and she didn't need to see the gleeful, derisive stares or the raised mandibles; she already knew what that looked like.

They would have lost her. If I hadn't acted, they would have lost her and more would have died.

It didn't matter. She'd branded herself an outsider yet again, shown herself to be unreliable by deserting her guard. It was ridiculous, it was a way of thinking that made no sense—

—and it is the Hunter's way.

Noguchi picked up her burner and waited for instruction, humiliated and furious, reminded yet again how very different she was from them—and that no matter how hard she tried, the Hunter's way seemed always beyond her reach.

They didn't like her—and she found out just how very much they wanted her gone when they got the queen back to the ship.

5

The call came just after Selee' had serviced him, a full rubdown front and back with a delicious finale; the girl's fine mouth and fingers drained the last of his travel tensions away better than a hot shower and a stim shot ever could, the suite's muted lighting and softly scented air giving the experience an air of privilege. Selee' had offered to bathe him afterward but Lucas Briggs knew better than to overindulge himself; he'd come to Zen's Respite for business rather than pleasure, and he'd do well not to let the two entwine—or not much, at least. He tipped her handsomely and had just seen her to the door when the vidscreen started to chime.

The coolly composed face on the screen belonged to Julia Russ, officially the Tri-Sec Communications Coordinator for Weyland/Yutani's DS900s. Unofficially, she was as ambitiously ruthless as she was brilliant, a renowned Company cannibal—and in direct competition with him for the next spot on the Applications Board. Not only was she a tremendous bitch, each meeting with her led him to believe that some women douched with liquid nitrogen. And found it too warm.

He smiled pleasantly, perfectly aware that having to report to him was torture for her; the loathing was entirely mutual, and Russ hadn't been informed about the 949 situation until late in the game.

Whereas I was there at the beginning, dear heart. Choke on it.

"Lucas. I see you're getting settled in," she said blandly, her pale blue gaze taking in the silken robe and mussed hair. "If this is an inconvenient time . . ."

"How nice of you to ask," he said, deliberately keeping his tone casual. If there was anything she hated, it was being taken lightly. "No, not at all. How are you, I haven't seen you since the last Earthside con. Keeping busy?"

Julia matched his smile, her eyes like chips of ice. "I'm well, thank you. I just received the numbers on our scan—"

"Don't tell me you've finished *already*," he interrupted. *My, isn't that adorable, you did your whole job just as quick as a tick!*

She gritted her teeth at him and continued. "—and the ST signal wasn't picked up, which suggests that the exo suit was taken from the site prior to the explosion. The spread pattern is such that my people aren't able to trace passage, but we should now assume that at least one member of the team managed to escape, taking the MAX with them."

The short range ST beacon couldn't be disabled, which meant that the MAX had been taken; someone had survived. It was what he'd hoped to hear, but he wasn't going to let her see it. "Yes, we expected as much," he said, stifling a deliberate yawn. "Any pickups on the *Nemesis*?"

"No. My field man believes it was destroyed; it's always possible that they disabled the tracking boards, but it's unlikely. We'll keep looking, of course, but I think all we can do now is wait to see where they set down. If they set down."

Briggs nodded. The joy of goading her was fizzling,

his thoughts already turning to where their runner might be headed. If the *Nemesis* had been lost, the suit must have been taken out on a shuttle or hopper—something small, or Julia's team would have spotted the trail. Disheartening news, considering how easy it was to disappear out in the DS sectors.

But an emergency craft isn't likely to get very far, either . . .

Zen's Respite was close to where 949 had been, less than three days on his Sun Jumper, and he'd come on the very slight possibility that someone on the *Nemesis* team might have made it out. Someone who'd had access to the *Trader's* log.

Someone who, if I can find them, if they have the information, and if I can make the deal, would absolutely assure my position with the Board.

"Worried about something, Lucas?" Julia asked sweetly.

Briggs frowned, tilting his head to one side. "Actually, yes. You've been to Zen's Respite recently . . . is Chin still cooking in the restaurant here? I heard rumor that he moved when the Company remodeled his kitchen."

If looks could maim. Julia's composure slipped for only a second, but the pure hatred that flickered across her features was truly a sight to behold. She reached forward and the screen went blank. Briggs grinned; not even a good-bye.

The pleasure was short-lived, quickly giving way to frustration. For a moment he sat and stared at the dead screen, searching for a way to hurry things along. He'd put Irwin and the guards on standby and double-check that the channels were all straight-lined to him . . .

. . . and wait. I can wait, and hope that they turn up somewhere Company or Company friendly, that the manager bothered to read the alert, and that whatever C4 channel jockey picks them up has the sense to report it.

A lot of ifs, a lot of hoping. Briggs sighed and stood up, already feeling like he needed another massage. He knew there was no point in worrying about it; they'd either turn up or they wouldn't, and he hadn't made it into the upper brackets of Weyland/Yutani by agonizing over things he couldn't control. And it wasn't as though Zen's Respite was such a bad place to wait. The Company's complex had four excellent restaurants, a full holovid rec room, and was within easy distance of a half dozen highly ranked organic gardens.

And there's the suite-level staff, of course. Selee' was able enough, but the brochure also listed several employees with skills and attributes that he wouldn't mind tasting. For 47 TS, he was in excellent shape, still perfectly capable of enjoying the satiation of his appetites. In fact, there was a particularly flexible young woman he'd heard about who could supposedly do things he'd only read about . . .

Briggs stretched his arms over his head and headed for the bathroom, deciding that he *would* relax; he always negotiated best when he was rested, and if—*when* the 949 fugitive turned up, he'd want to be fully prepared. Grigson had fumbled the ball and he'd been given the opportunity of a lifetime. If he pulled it off, he could write his own ticket. And if he fucked it up . . .

"Lucas Briggs does not fuck up," he said, his voice strong and even as he stepped into the elegant bathroom and tapped the shower to life. He didn't and wouldn't. Positive thinking, that was the key. And if his negotiation skills weren't enough to convince their wayward traveler, he'd resort to whatever method seemed appropriate.

Humming to himself, Briggs stripped and stepped into the steaming shower. And after a moment, he put a call in to the service staff and asked for that flexible young woman to join him.

As it turned out, she was able to make him forget all about DS 949, at least for a little while.

6

Noguchi led the Hunters back to the ship, assigned to the advance guard position; it was another slap, although not as bad as it could have been. Considering how angry Topknot had been, she supposed she should be grateful that he hadn't sent her ahead to open the dock; Shorty suffered that particular dishonor, and the look he gave her as he shoved past reminded Noguchi that she'd need to watch her back for a while.

The swarm of bugs moved out of the queen's path, falling back in ripples of hissing black. Noguchi walked slowly forward, determined to stay in position no matter what happened behind her—which, from the screams of the bound queen and the grunts of yautja exertion, was a heated struggle. It wasn't all that hard to ignore; the sight of hundreds, *thousands* of the chittering, trumpeting animals stepping aside to let them pass was an experience unlike any other. They parted like a living sea, smoothly sidling back, their heavy clawed feet tearing tracks in the muddy ground, the tracks filling with water and reflecting deadly darkness.

As they got closer to the ship, Noguchi started to breathe deeper, preparing herself for the probable conflict. The queen was smart enough to understand that boarding the ship wasn't what she wanted to be doing; Topknot had informed them that eight of ten queens taken as Hunt seeders tried to break away at the ramp, as soon as they realized that there wouldn't be another chance. Once the door was shut behind them, the danger was just as great; the queen might try to tear loose in a suicide run through the ship, forcing the yautja to take her out if she didn't fall for the "open" nest. The Hunters believed that, like themselves, a bug queen preferred death to captivity; having had her own experience with a rampaging queen, Noguchi agreed—although she also thought that the creature simply wanted to slaughter as many of her enemies as possible, whatever the consequences.

Which all means that we're not in the clear until she's nested and tied. The thought made her feel a little better about having been assigned to safer, less honorable positions for this Hunt. If the queen went into a frenzy once aboard, every Hunter shared responsibility for getting her back under control. Clan rules for Hunting were sacred, but they didn't apply to the ship—and that meant she had as much right as anyone to exhibit her skills.

Shorty had lowered the dock, the wide ramp settled in the marshy ground, a jutting mouth in the ship's swollen belly. Noguchi couldn't make the sounds that were the ship's name, and its twisting, bulbous shape defied simple description, but she thought it looked something like a seashell, sometimes thinking of it as *Shell*.

They were less than a dozen meters from the ramp, the ocean of sibilant drones hunched and watching blindly, their grins dripping strings of drool to the swampy ground. Noguchi was tensed, ready to spin around the instant she set foot on the ramp and there was no longer need for her position. When the queen made her move, she wasn't going to be caught off guard—

—and all at once the sea erupted, a thousand bugs throwing their heads back and screaming, the piercing cacophony shockingly painful—and as one, they leapt toward the band of Hunters, called to fight by some unseen signal from their dark mother.

Shit! The queen had chosen to risk the lives of her unborn against the lives of her own children—and had put the Hunters in a world of hurt.

She couldn't hear Topknot but was close enough to the ramp; one leap forward and her boot touched the ridged metal. She whipped around, firing into the oncoming horde, multiple blasts from the burner taking out three lunging drones in a single sweep.

From the edge of her vision, she saw only black darting bodies where the capture team had been—but the queen's comb was visible, tossing back and forth above the screaming onslaught. They still had her.

Everything happened too fast and too slow, fragments of action and the pulse of her heart twisting everything into flashes, *didn't expect this*—

Noguchi saw one, two of the young Hunters reach the platform, turning to fire, felt and saw the ship's covering blast, a lightning streak from above slamming a smoking hole through the brutal charge. The bass rumble was swallowed up by the shrill screams of the bugs, by the pounding of their running limbs against the wet ground.

She fired again and again as the battle raged, as the drones sacrificed themselves against the ragged wall of melting burner heat. Acid-splash hit the ramp and bubbled uselessly against the treated material—but not so ineffective against one of the young Hunters when his mask slipped or was torn away. Noguchi only saw the flailing arms and the blinded face, oozing green as the novice collapsed near her feet.

For some indeterminate time there was only the fight, the stink of burning muck and the strobe of the ship's weapons. Noguchi fired and backed up the ramp, fired, a step at a time, knowing that the mission objective still stood above all else. If the capture team could get the queen into the ship, Topknot would bring the ramp up. Anyone not aboard would be fucked, and honor or no, Noguchi didn't mean to die such a pointless death.

She was almost at the ship's wide-open dock, the heat and the strobe of the burner blasts from inside washing across the ramp, when she heard Topknot, his shrill, mechanically amplified whistle commanding the Hunters to look for him. The capture team had managed to get the bug queen to the bottom of the ramp and the Leader's raised, jerking fist meant it was time to board.

Still firing, Noguchi hustled backwards, saw the struggling team hauling their prize up to the ship—and saw that at least three of the novice Hunters weren't going to make it. They were too far away; unless they turned tail and sprinted for the ship, they were bug food. Even if the yautja culture allowed such cowardice, the young Hunters would be torn apart the second they stopped firing.

Honorable, they die with honor at least . . . The only consolation there was, that they would be remembered.

Halfway up the ramp, Topknot gave the command to close the dock. With *Shell* still firing into the horde, the wide slab of light metal pulled smoothly up into the ship, lifting the queen and her captors, Noguchi watching as the obedient drones continued to throw themselves into certain death. As the ramp closed, she caught a last glimpse of the doomed trio, still blasting away at the trumpeting assault.

The queen's furious cry seemed like a whisper after the screams of so many, but the desperate rage carried—

—and Noguchi saw that what was left of the team wouldn't be able to hold her. Two of the rope holders were gone, a third badly wounded, barely able to stand. The attack was a surprise, the queen's decision to use her children to save herself unprecedented, at least as far as Noguchi knew—and the Hunters hadn't been prepared. In all, six of the thirteen queen Hunters had been lost.

Topknot was clattering at the remnants of his group, calling for the nest hatch to be opened, calling for the untrained yautja to get out of the way as he snatched at one of the loose ropes, dropping his burner.

Noguchi sidled backwards toward the nesting room, watching the queen pull and strain at her bonds as the Hunters brought her under control. The "nest," a massive, heavily reinforced chamber designed to hold the bug mother, wasn't far from the dock opening, thirty meters of bare floor between the two doors. The Hunters had designed the lowest levels of their seeding ships with bug behavior in mind; with her exit back to the planet's surface blocked, she should willingly go into the nest, the only direction left for her. Once trapped inside, she would be lured to the back of the chamber and temporarily restrained by hanging ropes, until the yautja could bind her more permanently— she'd be strapped to a wall, gagged and shackled, as helpless to the Hunters as she was to her own biological drives. An egg-layer, bearing seeds for the Hunt for as long as the yautja wanted her.

Most of the observation windows were small and filtered, the queen seeming to prefer darkness for nesting, but the main hatch had a wide oblong, clear as glass. A spot next to the door would also mean that the captured queen would be passing close enough for Noguchi to touch—

—except they couldn't keep her. Noguchi was only a few meters from the open hatch when she glanced back and saw that Scar had lost his grip. She saw it and then saw the wounded Hunter, a novice she called Slats, drop his own rope and crumple to the deck.

Next to her, a surprised hiss, an untrained yautja
diving away from the hatch controls—

—and the freed queen screamed, ripping the last
ropes away from the team, fixing her sightless, slaver-
ing face toward the opening not ten meters in front of
her. The nest, where they wanted her to go.

Where Noguchi stood, blocking her path.

She automatically raised the burner as the queen
lunged forward. A few well-placed bursts and—

—can't—

Noguchi threw the burner, the queen close enough
for her to see the bubbles in her dripping string of saliva, see the stainless teeth of her inner jaws snap—

—and *crunch* on the weapon's thickness. Noguchi
spun and ran into the chamber, the close sounds of
rending metal lending her speed. Her racing thoughts,
her plans, were shadowed by a burst of self-disgust as
she tore through the humid, echoing dark of the nest.

Run run circle left goddamn honor—

Killing the queen would have been easy—and it
would have made the deaths of the other Hunters a
waste, and she couldn't even blame their strange culture for her decision. This was her own honor at stake.

Noguchi sprinted, arms pumping, fully aware that
the queen was faster. All she heard was the thunder of
the animal's pursuit, all she felt was the knot of ice in
her belly, the inner flinch of each heartbeat that told
her she would be jerked into the air and hurled into
blackness before she even felt the pain—

—*now now NOW!*

She could *feel* the air sliced behind and above and
she threw herself left, tucking smoothly into a shoulder
roll and coming up running, not looking back.

The queen shrieked, a terrible sound but one that
filled Noguchi's every fiber with a kind of restrained relief. The enormous bug mother was fast but heavy, unable to change direction easily; the frustrated cry came
from near the back of the giant chamber and Noguchi

was already halfway back to the door, only twenty meters—

—almost, almost there and she's trapped—

—and when she saw Topknot step into the opening, a flush of pride added length to her strides, her heart pounding with more than just adrenaline. She'd done the right thing, acted as bravely as any Blooded Hunter—

—and so sure was she that her prowess would finally be acknowledged by the Leader, she mistook his signal for one of celebration, a twist of talon that meant "victory." It wasn't until she actually saw the silhouette of the Leader disappearing, saw the ring of faces appear at the window and heard the massive, resounding *whoom* of the hatch slamming down that she realized what had happened.

Topknot *had* signaled victory, but not to Noguchi. And behind her, the queen signaled her own triumph, a scream of bloodlust that pounded at Noguchi even as her ringing, shuddering footfalls pounded at the floor.

7

". . . this message. Repeat: this is the shuttle from the Weyland/Yutani ship *Nemesis*, requesting emergency assistance from any ship or outpost receiving this message . . ."

Ellis's soft voice droned on, carrying back to where the Max rested, to where Lara and Jess drifted silently. The young tech had been at it for almost three hours and still managed to sound hopeful, as if he believed his voice might actually reach farther than the distress beacon. As if with each pause, he expected to hear a reply.

"Anyone listening would've picked up our code hours ago," Jess said quietly, a touch of concern in his deep voice. Lara was glad to hear it; maybe it was selfish on her part, but Jess had tuned in again and it was a relief to have him back.

She shrugged. "Let him talk, if it makes him feel better."

Jess sighed. "Yeah. What the hell, right?"

Rhetorical. Lara nodded anyway, wondering if the time was right to bring up what she'd been thinking about. With both men so fragile, she'd been hesitant to talk about the specifics of what needed to be done—but she knew that she didn't want to spend her last minutes of consciousness trying to breathe, and she needed to know what position they would take.

I can do myself, but they might need help, Ellis, anyway. And is either of them strong enough to watch if I'm the only one wanting to sign out early?

"Still got Pop's standard issue?"

Lara blinked, then nodded again. It seemed that she wasn't the only one considering their options.

"Twelve rounds," she said, before he could ask.

Jess looked at her, and she was grateful to see how composed he was. "Talked to Ellis yet?"

"Not yet." Lara smiled a little. "There's not really any casual way to slip it into a conversation."

Jess grinned suddenly, his gaze glittering with humor that she'd thought he'd lost. "Oh, I don't know. How 'bout, 'So, got any plans for how you wanna buy it? I hear getting shot's not so bad; pass the coffee, wouldya?'"

Lara was surprised into an actual giggle. It was a small sound, but it made her feel a hell of a lot better—and she thought that if she had to go anyway, at least her final hours would be with someone like Martin Jess. Whatever he'd done in the past, he was a good man.

"Want me to talk to him?" Jess asked, his smile fading.

Lara shook her head. "I can do it. Might as well wait a little longer, though. He's . . . he's still got *hope*, you know?"

He knew. She could see it in the dark depths of his eyes. Hope was a fleeting thing, something that shouldn't be ripped away before it had a chance to dwindle on its own. She was only a few years older than Ellis, but like Jess, she had no illusions about their situation; if Ellis was still able to find comfort in his, she didn't want to deny him that.

"Do you think they're looking for us?" Jess asked. "For that download?"

There was a thread of anger in his voice that she hadn't heard before. "I don't know. Doesn't matter, does it?"

Jess shrugged. "I guess not. I'm—I gotta admit, I wouldn't mind running into a Company crew right about now, and not just to save our butts."

His tone was mild but his eyes narrowed, the set of his jaw and the tic high on his cheek telling her more perhaps than he wanted to reveal. "Fuck 'em, right?"

Definitely anger, and he meant it. Lara nodded slowly, thinking that misplaced hope wasn't the only thing that could keep someone going.

Ellis has his rescue dreams, and it seems that Jess has revenge . . .

"I'm gonna go see how he's holding up," Jess said, and moved away, leaving Lara alone. Leaving her wondering what *she* had, what was keeping her from collapse.

"I'm a goddamn *Marine*," she mumbled, the soft words filling her with an odd mix of amusement, embarrassment and pride. Out of practice maybe, running transmission lines on a corporate payroll, but the Corps was the Corps; as the saying went, she didn't get to die without permission.

Semper fi, sir, yes sir. Not much, maybe, but it beats the hell out of feeling sorry for myself.

It'd do. Lara mentally squared her shoulders and headed up to the front, Ellis's soft voice still droning on, his words surely disappearing, unheard, into the blank waves of emptiness that would be their tomb.

Briggs liked to think of himself as a thoughtful man, but the garden so originally titled "Sand" was peaceful to the point of coma-inducing. He sat on a small stone bench at the edge of a vast, carefully raked field of white grit, wondering what genius had marketed a giant sandbox as art. He could understand the appeal, he supposed, if one liked staring at waves of lines and contemplating "beingness," but he wasn't that one.

Briggs glanced at his watch and then sighed, gazing back out at the flat, featureless sea. He'd have to give it another ten or fifteen minutes. Heiro Fujiyami probably wouldn't bother looking at Briggs's Respite itinerary, but it would be well worth an hour of boredom if he did; Sand was Fujiyami's favorite, and his vote would carry at least two of the others along when it came time for the Board to elect their new member.

Still . . .

Another sigh. It was *sand*, nice patterns but not even a rock or tree to break the monotony. Twilight was settling, a cool purple light bathing the bland garden, at least giving it a *color*. He'd have to treat himself afterward, perhaps a nice dinner at the seafood place near the suites. They grew catfish there, killed to order and fried with cornmeal; heavy, but he deserved some reward—

The bleat of his 'com was a welcome distraction. Briggs slipped the handset from his breast pocket and hit the receive.

"Mr. Briggs, this is Nirasawa," the bodyguard's smooth voice rumbled. "You have a call from Mr. Terrence Roth, on behalf of Ms. Julia Russ, Tri-Sec Communications Coordinator for—"

"Yes, put him through," Briggs snapped. Nirasawa was more efficient than Keene, but only physically. He seemed determined to fit as much formality as possible into each and every sentence.

There was a short pause, enough time for Briggs to remember that Roth was the name of Julia's field scout, before a low, tentative voice sounded in his ear.

"Mr. Briggs? Ah, Ms. Russ asked me to call you if I, if we picked up anything on that possible fugitive situation. She said you could contact her if you wanted any more help. *Information*," he amended hastily. "Anything besides what I picked up. What *we* picked up."

He was rattled. Some low level, undoubtedly aware

of the animosity between Julia and himself. Briggs
smoothed his tone; if she wasn't actually listening in,
she'd certainly be recording the conversation. "I appreciate your call, Mr. Roth. And excellent work . . . you
say you've found something?"

"Yeah," Roth said, obviously relieved that he
wasn't going to be skewered by his boss's nemesis. "Sir.
We caught the distress signal for, uh, ETTC-C *Nemesis*,
shuttle six-oh-nine-one-oh, far edge of Sector 955."

Got you!

Briggs forced a calm he didn't feel, grinning out at
the field of sand. "Really? That's wonderful. Do you
know their status?"

"They're out of fuel . . . and unless someone on
Nemesis stocked the shuttle up with extra oxy filters,
they've gotta be low on air. I'd say they were out, but
Ms. Russ told me that there might be a couple of techs
on board, they could've stacked the screens . . ."

Briggs gritted his teeth, reminding himself that Irwin could have the ship ready to go in five minutes as
Roth droned on for another few seconds about the me-
chanics of air filtration. They could be on their way in
ten.

*Far edge of 955, there's that survey outpost on—Bud-
dha? Bandy? Thirty, thirty-five hours, tops. Have Keene look
up the head there, probably some bio geek, make sure they
read the goddamn memo—*

". . . and then the cross weave'd give 'em another
ten, maybe twelve hours. Anyway. Ms. Russ said that
you'd want to be informed before any decisions were
made—"

"—and I thank you for your promptness, Mr.
Roth," Briggs said. "Please tell Julia that I'll handle
things from here. And that I'll contact her just as soon
as I need her input." He accented *need*, grinning again.

*Perhaps I can call to get her opinion on what to wear,
my first week on the Board . . .*

Roth quickly signed off and Briggs stood as he
punched Nirasawa's number, turning away from the ri-

diculously dull garden and talking as he walked. He was in his element, now that there was something solid to work with; over the koi pond and past the authentically shabby tearoom, motioning to Keene who stood stiffly by the front entrance and giving instruction to Nirasawa, Briggs felt full of anticipation, of excitement for things to come. No more waiting, hoping, ifing . . .

Someone from the MAX team had survived. And if they knew anything about the download from the *Trader*, he was going to get it.

8

She was trapped in the dark with an alien queen.

The panic lasted less than a second and then Noguchi's skills took over, natural and learned, honed from her year with the predatory race. Without a misstep, Noguchi veered away from the closed hatch, as sharply as she could without losing speed, ignoring the circle of watching masks outside. Some part of her saw that Shorty was at the center of the window, a part that apparently assumed she'd survive and might at some point care, but that awareness was gone a split second later; her animal brain was more concerned with saving her skin than with her need to save face.

The echo of the queen's closing scream blasted through the heated dark, stealing the usual calm certainty Noguchi had so often achieved in battle—that she would survive and her enemy would not. She was scared, but a veteran of many scary places; her mind fed her what she needed to know as she sprinted, arms pumping, her face flushed with her own terrified breath reflected as heat by her mask. The suit's shoulder burner was too small to do more than scratch the queen, there were no weapons to run for, hand-to-hand was less than possible. She had to get out, fast, and there was only the hatch—

—*hatch and nothing hatch and where she's supposed to be tied up*—

The restraints. Near the back of the nest, the lowest dangling two meters off the floor—two chains and a rope, hanging just beneath the air shaft that blew humid heat across the nesting wall. They'd be looped around the queen's comb and throat once the queen got hungry enough to investigate the carrion pile underneath, maneuvered by controls from outside.

It had taken her less than a half dozen running steps away from the front hatch to consider all of her options and decide. Only five or six meters to climb and a metal grate to burn through at the shaft's opening, only seconds to do it—but with nearly a thousand kilos of screaming alien death bearing down on her from behind, even a stupid plan was better than no plan at all.

Noguchi didn't look but could hear her over her own hot, sharp gasps and the rapid fire of her heart. The queen had turned to give chase, the floor trembling in time to the demonic echoes of pursuit that surrounded them.

Sweating but somehow cold, Noguchi struck out for the northeast corner of the chamber; she'd have to outmaneuver the queen again, feint right and go left before the mammoth creature could stop herself from slamming into the wall.

Her feelings of fear, of pain and of death, had no hold. Noguchi saw the heavy shadows of the corner, pounding closer, felt her muscles flex and pump, calculated distances and times. Behind her, the thunder of steps grew louder.

Another leap, another, the sharp lines of darkness a meter away, Noguchi shifted her weight and pivoted at once. For one sideways, running step, her left foot

was on the ground, her right angled against the back
wall—

—and she'd sprinted only two steps when the crash
came. The queen hit the wall close enough for a spatter
of her flinging drool to hit the back of Noguchi's neck.
She found her second wind as the sliver of hot, viscous
foam crawled down her spine, as close to panic as she
could allow.

Fasterfaster!

To her right now, the seamless stretch of dark
metal wall, ahead and to her right a shade of empty
blackness, broken by slashes of filtered light from observation slits. Hunter masks had infrared capability although they rarely used it, the bugs didn't radiate
heat—but she'd long ago disabled hers, confused by the
yautja symbols that flashed across the field of view;
now, she wished she hadn't, running blind. No more
than twenty meters, surely, she had to be getting
close—

—there! The dull glint of metal, motionless and
slender, two meters up. Noguchi stretched her arms up
and out, tensed as she took her final leaping step—

—and *fuck that hurts*, pulled, swinging herself
around the thick and leaden chain by one aching arm,
the other hand already reaching for the next hold. The
heavy links barely swayed, Noguchi's feet in the air,
and the *bam, bam* of the queen's pursuit too close.

Hand over hand, Noguchi flew up the chain, climbing so fast that she barely felt the rough metal brushing
against her legs or the sheath of sweat that dripped beneath her armor. She could already feel the blast of
moist air coming from the rounded tunnel to her left
and above, running parallel to the ceiling. Two meters,
one, and Noguchi was facing the mesh grate that
blocked her escape.

Gripping the chain with her right hand, she leaned
back and hooked her left arm, aiming for the center of
the screen. The stream of brilliant blue light from the
small shoulder weapon smashed through the holed

metal, twigs of the heated mesh hissing to the wet floor of the shaft. She was so close, both hands on the tunnel—

—and when the queen's skeletal fingers slid into her hair, she didn't hesitate, didn't think about extending her right hand's blades and reaching over her own shoulder to cut. The thin, impossibly hard knives that shot out from the forearm mechanism worked as claws, slicing as easily through braided, beaded hair as through the bony dusk of the queen's talons—

—and even as the enraged, agonized shriek assaulted Noguchi's ears, she had boosted herself into the tunnel before she realized that she was free. As quickly as it had begun, it was over. Below, the queen screamed on as Noguchi scrambled forward, elbowing through the warm, humid dark back toward the landing dock, the awareness of what had happened seeping in.

She had me. She touched me.

And yet Noguchi was alive, unharmed, while the alien breeder bled acid, at least three of her long digits slashed away. The rush of light and energy that swept through her as she crawled the last few meters of shaft was as exhilarating and beautiful as only victory could be.

Victory, narrow but true and well deserved. And with all of them watching . . .

With the alien's hollow howls fading behind, she could consider the others. With only a few exceptions, everyone on *Shell* would have seen the incident, Blooded and novice alike, an infrared show of her prowess. They couldn't continue to ignore her, the training group would have to cease their blatantly derisive treatment of her—they'd probably never like her, but there would at last be some bare minimum of respect.

Noguchi saw the curve ahead in the close air shaft, muted light shining up in thin lines around a floor hatch. She grinned, high from being alive and capable, hearing the Hunters shifting restlessly below as she popped the edge of the hatch.

She touched me, you impassive bastards, you can't pretend that there's no honor in walking away from that. Can't.

The drop was only four meters, the hatch directly over a high, sloping storage rack. Noguchi landed in a crouch, then hopped lightly to the floor, not ten meters from the front hatch of the nest chamber. Topknot and Minikui and Tress and Shorty, the wounded Scar, all of them stood and looked at her, silent, masks still in place. For a moment, there was no movement at all.

Noguchi grinned again, reaching up to pop the line that connected her mask to her armor. A tiny hiss of escaping air and the normal heat of the ship seemed like a cool breeze across the sweat on her skin, the dull light too bright for a few blinks.

The line of masks watched her, not speaking, Topknot in front. The others would look to their Leader for an appropriate response, and he couldn't punish her after such a competent display . . .

Topknot didn't. Noguchi gritted her teeth as he turned away instead, reaching up to take off his own mask as he growled an order to one of the unBlooded, to see to Slats. Randomly, one by one, the Hunters all turned away. They removed masks, moved to store them, shelved burners, and clattered to one another about those lost and how many they'd killed, their crablike faces shiny with musk, their beaded tresses slick with it. No one spoke to her and there was nothing spoken about her.

Noguchi didn't, wouldn't care. The mission was complete, she was alive, and they had all seen what she'd done, whether or not it was acknowledged. It wasn't hard to feel nothing; she'd had so much practice, for so long . . .

. . . *but it was a* queen, she thought, a small and pitiful thought that she immediately buried. Instead, she hung her mask and peeled her gloves, her head high and shoulders back, wondering how much longer she could stand to live this way.

He'd been talking for a long time, the repeated message forming a kind of circle in his mind; it had gone past hope, past despair, and now was a meditation, a soothing message of possibility in a voice that he no longer recognized as his.

. . . *this is the Weyland/Yutani ship* Nemesis *request emergency assistance from any ships or outposts receiving this message* . . .

Lara and Jess had both wandered up, sat for a while, wandered away. Ellis kept talking, pausing, talking, and had become so lulled by his vocal loop that he was annoyed when a crackle of harsh static interrupted him. But only for the fraction of a second it took him to realize that someone was answering.

"*Nemesis* shuttle, this is Bunda survey, we read you four-by-four. Please state the nature of your emergency and adjust your BD signal to channel eleven-oh-one-dash-one, over."

A man's voice, mild but tight with a barely hidden excitement. A *person*, a young-sounding man with the clipped tones of a Company-trained channel checker. Ellis stared at the mike pad on the console in front of him, at the speaker filter next to it, astounded by how suddenly things had changed.

We're not lost anymore.

"Repeat, this is Bunda survey, *Nemesis* shuttle, do you read?"

"Jesus, keep 'im talking, Ellis!" Jess said, suddenly floating next to him, looking as shocked as Ellis felt. Lara was right behind him, her eyes wide and fixed.

"Ah, we read you, Bunda," he stammered, "we're—we're going to be out of oxy in, less than ten hours. And we're out of fuel already—oh, *shit*—"

Ellis started to laugh, turning to see the same dawning expressions on both of their faces. They weren't going to die, they had been lost and now some man from Bunda was asking them questions.

Lara pushed forward, grinning, taking over. "What was that channel again, Bunda?"

Leaning in front of Ellis she tapped keys and Jess gripped his shoulder firmly, laughing with him.

"You did it, Ellis, go fuckin' figure. First the Max, now this—they're gonna have to promote you, kid." Jess shook his shoulder gently, trying to keep his voice low as Lara called up Bunda's stats and info and spoke to their savior.

Savior—as Ellis had been when he and Max had joined at the station. As he was now, having found that voice from out of the dark.

Ellis laughed harder, warm and giddy, feeling the positive waves that radiated from Lara and Jess. From their *team*.

Twice. Twice, and it's not a fluke if it happens more than once.

Because of him, everything had changed. Again. It was a feeling he could get used to. Maybe he wasn't destined to be a tech geek, working his life away in some sterile hydraulics lab. And really, wasn't it a career he'd chosen out of fear? His scrawny build, his lack of self-confidence, and feelings of inadequacy had led him to choose a quiet, stable, boring line of work. Even signing up with a volunteer team had seemed wildly dangerous, and the job description was watching monitors and pushing buttons . . .

. . . *and look where I've ended up. Everything has changed, is changing, will change and all because of me and Max, 72.43 minutes eradicated 122 adult species dot 47 embryonic—*

Ellis had a headache suddenly.

"Hey, kid, you okay?"

He looked up into Jess's smiling, slightly worried face and forced a grin. "Fine, yeah. We're outa here, right?"

Jess clapped him on the shoulder again, turning his

attention back to Lara—and leaving Ellis to wonder why he hadn't told the truth. Being with Max had done something to him, clouded his thinking, Lara and Jess both knew it . . .

. . . *and maybe I'm ready for them to see me as a man, now, strong, not whining about my little aches and pains* . . .

On some level, he knew better. The dual prongs of the Max's interface had gone into his brain, far from a little wound. If they were going to work together, shouldn't he tell them that he was still having flashes of, of *altered* thinking?

Ellis considered it for only 6.6 seconds, until Lara glanced back at him from the console. The warm look she gave him decided it; he wasn't going to be pitied, ever again. He could control himself, he could bear the pain—and whatever else there was to bear.

Besides, they were safe now. A survey station, scientists and biotechs probably; no aliens, no Company, no *death*.

For some unfathomable reason, that thought gave him no comfort at all.

9

One of the few advantages to being different was that she had been given private quarters, a luxury that was only afforded to the strongest and most aggressive of the older Hunters. The un-Blooded slept on mats in a giant chamber Noguchi thought of as "the pit," their every spare moment spent watching fights or participating in them. Most training ships only carried a dozen or so novices, but *Shell* housed up to forty young males, making the pit an exercise in arrogant posturing.

Noguchi sat on the edge of her makeshift bed and took off her boots, feeling wrung out and depressed, not wanting to think about what had happened in the dock. The small, dark room that she called home was the only place she really felt at ease anymore, the few mementos from her past giving her some small measure of peace. A medkit, a few toiletries, an aging wave scanner. There was a photo of Creep tacked to one wall, the dog that had stayed with her on Ryushi after the colonists had left. Before she'd gone with the Hunters, she'd sent a signal to the closest outpost, requesting a pickup. She wondered where the friendly mutt was now, if he'd ever been reunited with his previous owner . . .

The thought made her feel like crying and she looked away from the hard-copy picture, looked up at the mammoth crowned skull that dominated the room from its place over her bed. The queen that she and Broken Tusk had killed, together. It was her first trophy, and she'd kept it with her on Ryushi, spent long, silent hours gazing at it, dreaming of the spiritual trek that awaited her when the Hunters finally came. She'd imagined living among a people that found enlightenment in pushing beyond their own physical limits, a race that found life and self-awareness in the honorable death of a parasitic breed. Two years she'd waited, alone on the hot and barren world except for Creep and a few head of rhynth; she knew that one day they'd appear, looking for their missing ship. And when they came, she'd go with them, embarking on a journey unlike any other . . .

That wasn't a happy thought either, not anymore. Noguchi leaned back on the hard cot and crossed her legs, trying to come up with something that didn't make her hurt.

Past is over. Think of the future, not of what's already gone. It was a strong thought, a positive one, and it worked as long as she didn't remind herself that she relied on it constantly. Some days, it seemed to be all she had.

Except for the Hunt. The queen had been secured and was already producing eggs, which meant two days or less until the next one. It was going to be big, too; she'd gathered as much from the excited chatter of the novices on her way to her quarters. A big Hunt was something to look forward to, and this one sounded as important as any she'd participated in since coming to live with the yautja. Several well respected Hunters would rendezvous with *Shell*, Leader and warrior alike, and the novices would finally be given their marks, which meant many of them would move on. Blooding, the etched mark of a Leader on his student's forehead, was the sign that a teacher believed his trainee was trustworthy to Hunt alone.

She reached up and touched the jagged scar above the bridge of her nose, unable to stop herself from thinking about Broken Tusk. Dachande was his yautja name, but the curved tooth of his lower left mandible had been snapped off, and she still thought of him by the description.

Maybe things would have been different if he'd lived. Maybe we'd still be Hunting together . . .

Not necessarily true. They'd been thrown together under unusual circumstances, to say the least; if they'd met somewhere, anywhere else, perhaps her skull would be a trophy on *his* wall now.

She sighed, shaking her head. She didn't believe that. Dachande had been a warrior of integrity and skill, and had respected her enough to Blood her, his final act before dying. They'd saved each other multiple times on that endless, bloody night so long ago. And she'd been so impressed, so changed by the experience that she'd chosen to join with his people. Who were so unlike him, she no longer knew what she was going to do.

There it was, the truth of it. Noguchi rolled over on one side, pulling her knees up, feeling an ache deep in her gut. After a lifetime of carefully building up defenses and learning how hurtful people could be, she'd rejected her own kind in favor of a race she knew nothing about. In her steady climb up the Chigusa corporate ladder, she'd been called an ice queen, frigid, a robot—and on some level, the mean-spirited tags had been accurate. She didn't really *like* people—

—and so I gave them up. For this.

She couldn't discount the powerfully addictive thrill of the Hunt—but she also couldn't keep telling herself that things were going to get better. She was tolerated, no more; no one had even tried to teach her anything beyond the most basic of yautja language, and she felt even more alone than when she'd been the sole human being on Ryushi. At least then, she'd had her dreams.

Impulsively, she reached out to the wave scanner next to the bed and tapped it on. The obsolete hunk of machinery was set to a search pattern, and started lisping out static as she lay back down, reaching out into the universe for a channel in use. For months upon months, she hadn't touched the scanner, not even sure why she'd dragged it along; it couldn't transmit far enough to bother with, and didn't receive much better. But in the last few weeks, she'd been turning it on more and more. Sometimes, not often, she'd catch a word or two in English or Japanese—and that contact, insignificant as it was, soothed her.

With the soft hiss of blankness washing through the tiny room, Noguchi closed her eyes, finally allowing herself to think about what had happened and what it meant. She'd been berated for saving the mission the first time, in the nest, and ignored for her efforts to help trap the queen once aboard. If one of the Hunters had escaped the queen's clutches, he would have commanded a new respect; had it been a novice, he might even have been Blooded.

Not an ooman, though. Not some tiny, pale, alien female. Doesn't matter that I carry Dachande's mark, or the name he gave me, doesn't matter that I joined the Hunters with a trophy that most Leaders don't even hope for—

". . . quest emergency . . . om any . . . receiving . . ."

A young man's voice, barely audible through the blank spots and hissing static, whispered into the small room. Noguchi tensed, straining to make out the message.

". . . peat . . . land/Yutani . . . mesis . . ."

Weyland/Yutani, a name she hadn't thought of in years. The Company.

She caught the word, "Repeat," clear as day, and

then there was a sharp, crackling pop—and the soft
voice was gone. There was no way to know how long
the message had been out there before her scanner had
picked it up; maybe hours, maybe days. Maybe the
sender had succumbed to his emergency and was already dead.

Like me, she thought, and finally, the tears came.
Noguchi curled into herself and let them fall, wondering where there was left for her to go.

Six hours after Ellis made contact with the outpost, a
D-Ship tractored them in and passed over enough fuel
and air to last them to the surface. The fuel wasn't a
problem, but D-Ships weren't designed to lend air to
anything as small as an ETTC shuttle. Lucky for them,
the ship's pilot was clever enough to have adapted one
of their locks with an aperture compression tunnel; five
minutes after the hookup, the shuttle's filters were
clean, the weaves revitalized, the air changing from
stale and dead to amazingly sweet.

Company air. In a just universe, it would smell like shit.

Lara was piloting, Ellis was asleep again, and Jess
was trying to come to terms with who they were following. He sat stiffly next to Lara, hands in his lap, the
smoldering anger in his gut making it impossible to
rest. A Weyland/Yutani D-Ship for a Company survey
outpost. Didn't it just fucking figure.

At least they'd had those six hours to feel good, to
feel grateful to whatever God had seen fit to spare them
yet again; it wasn't until the D-Ship made contact that
they found out. The channel jockey, a man named
Windy, had neglected to mention Bunda's affiliation.
In fact, the obviously nervous Mr. Windy hadn't given
them much at all, besides coordinates and ETAs, and
that worried Jess as much as anything. It was a Company planet, only a survey station, researchers and
such, but still part of the same system that had so thoroughly screwed them.

Before his well deserved death, Pop had made it

clear that Grigson—the exec in charge of volunteer Max teams—had sent them in to 949 to get a log from one of the docked ships, the Company *Trader*. And that once the data was retrieved, it was up to Pop to get rid of everyone who knew that the *Trader* had been the source of the alien outbreak.

Grigson sent the orders, but there was no chance in hell he was acting on his own. No chance.

"They probably figure we're dead anyway," Lara said quietly.

Jess smiled, just a little. After so much time stuck together, they seemed to be on the same wavelength.

"Yeah," he said. "Except we're not, and I figure they probably sent a heads up to every post in this half of the big black, just in case. You heard how Windy was."

Lara nodded slowly, keeping her tired gaze fixed on the nav screen. They were trail hooked to the D-Ship, nothing for her to do, but she was as by-the-book as they came; if even one number read was off, she'd be all over it.

"Right," she sighed. "So, any ideas?"

Jess shrugged. "See how it looks once we set down, I guess. I mean, we worked for 'em, and didn't know how fucked they were; maybe it's the same for this group. If we tell them what happened, they might help us."

"Assuming we can get them to believe us," Lara said.

He nodded. "And assuming they haven't already sent word back to the suits . . ."

Of course they had, but he didn't need to tell her that. The security on Bunda probably already had orders to kill them . . .

. . . except why bother saving our asses out here, if they just mean to off us on landing?

The Max, maybe; it was an expensive piece of equipment—except it would be just as easy to salvage that after their air ran out. Funny, how complicated things got when one found out that they weren't going to die after all . . .

"Jess, you think there was something on that log? Besides proof that it was the Company's fuckup?"

He snorted. "Isn't that enough? Killing four hundred of their own is plenty, you ask me."

Lara finally looked away from the screen, frowning. "Grigson wanted that download and he wanted us dead, right? So if Bunda already told the Company that they found us, why wouldn't they just leave us out here to die, unless—"

"—unless they think maybe we hid the download," Jess finished.

They sat in silence for a moment, the quiet hum of the shuttle's systems interrupted only by Ellis's occasional snore from the back. They could knock themselves out trying to guess what the Company did or didn't want, what information had been exchanged about the remnants of their team, whether or not they were slated for torture, death, or a vacation; what it came down to was that they wouldn't know until they knew.

"We wait," Jess said finally, scruffing at the stubble on his chin. "Wait and see what's what. We thank whoever's calling the shots for pulling us in, get Ellis to a med program, hit the showers, and just—just wait and see."

Not the most comforting of answers, but it was the best he could do. Lara was together enough to handle herself, whatever came up; Ellis, on the other hand . . . physically, he was a lot better, but Jess wasn't sure how he was doing otherwise. There was a vague look in his eyes now that wasn't there before his sacrificial ride in the Max. And he sometimes talked about the suit like—well, like it was more than a suit.

Gonna have to watch out for him. . . . The kid had saved his life, and tried to save Teape and Pulaski; Jess wasn't about to let anything happen to him.

"Looking at—ETA five hours, twenty minutes," Lara said. "About 1100 on Bunda."

In just before lunch. Jess tried to think of some clever comment to go with the news, but he was too wasted. He really should try to get a little more sleep—except they were going to land in the middle of Company in just a few hours, and that thought cinched the knot of rage in his belly. No way he could sleep.

That they were basically unarmed, exhausted, and outnumbered didn't make a difference. If the biotechs on Bunda didn't know how fucked the Company was, he was going to make sure they fully understood the situation. And if they did know, if they embraced the avarice and treachery of Weyland/Yutani with open arms . . .

. . . *then they're gonna be sorry they ever picked up our call. Real sorry.*

Jess sighed inwardly, wondering when he'd become such an optimist. Whatever happened next, it wasn't going to be up to him.

10

According to the files that Nirasawa had pulled, the head paper pusher on Bunda wasn't used to dealing with execs; Kevin Vincent was a botanist who'd been moved into admin by pure happenstance, a chart watcher for the thirty-plus techs on the small planet. Considering Vincent had made the monumental error of letting one of his people answer the *Nemesis* shuttle's CDS, Briggs couldn't be more pleased with the circumstances; in his experience, scientists were a mostly spineless bunch, and Vincent wouldn't know that the mistake was a minor one—or that Briggs had been aware of the situation since well before the contact had been made. With as long as the shuttle had been drifting, there was no chance of infection, but Briggs didn't want anyone to meet with the survivors before he did.

He grinned, looking forward to meeting Vincent and exercising his persuasive skills. The man would be under his thumb in less than a minute.

Nirasawa silently brought him a drink while Keene put in the call, the beverage as much for effect as anything. A suit holding a cocktail would scare the shit out of a botanist stationed someplace like Bunda.

"Mr. Briggs?" The granite-faced Keene had stepped into the cabin, his massive frame tucked into a tailor-made suit, a brown so dark it was almost black. The equally bulky Nirasawa was dressed the same; Briggs liked the look of a matched set.

Briggs nodded, tapping the connect key on the contoured wall unit, leaning back in his chair and taking a sip of his drink. A thin-faced man, 40 TS or so with straggly blond hair, peered into the cabin.

"Mr. Briggs?" Vincent was already scared; Briggs could see the sweat on his upper lip, the high-res screen showing him each beaded droplet in perfect clarity. "I'm Kevin Vincent, ASM377, Bunda survey—"

"I know who you are," Briggs said. "And I understand you contacted a shuttle from *Nemesis* before you alerted the home office . . ."

He leaned forward, setting the drink down and staring coldly at the nervous Vincent. ". . . and that you've already sent assistance to this shuttle. Is this accurate information?"

Vincent nodded rapidly, talking to match it. "Yes, sir, the A1 didn't say anything about not talking to anyone in distress and my crew put in a call immediately to—"

"Yes, I understand all that," Briggs said. "What *you* don't understand is how extremely delicate this matter is, and how continued . . . *mismanagement* of this situation might result in some rather severe consequences."

Vincent looked miserable, and said nothing.

Time for the push . . .

Briggs lifted his glass again, relaxing his tone. "Earthside wants me to handle this personally, but I'm still twelve hours away, give or take." The shuttle would set down in just under three. "Tell me . . . can I trust that the Company will have your full cooperation?"

Vincent couldn't answer quickly enough. "Yes, sir. Everyone—whatever you need, our entire operation is at your disposal."

Briggs nodded. "Fine, that's fine. I want the shuttle quarantined, no one in or out, and no interaction between your staff and the people on board, physical or verbal."

Vincent nodded, swallowing heavily before speaking. "Uh . . . there may be someone in need of medical attention, Mr. Briggs."

Briggs knew that already, knew everything that had passed between the shuttle and Bunda. Three people were on board—a communications tech on contract, a volunteer ground-squad leader, and a MAX Doc. The MAX tech, a Brian K. Ellis, had been injured somehow.

"No interaction," he repeated, in a voice that promised death and destruction to anyone stupid enough to disobey. "Do you understand?"

"Yes, sir."

Briggs smiled coldly. "Then we have nothing more to discuss."

Vincent nodded, finally wiping the sweat from his face with the back of one hand. "Yes, sir. I'll have our LZ coordinates sent to—"

Briggs tapped the disconnect before he could finish, satisfied that his instructions would be followed to the letter. With nonexec types, fear was usually the best motivator, especially with scientists. All Vincent wanted now was to get Briggs the hell away from Bunda as quickly as possible, so that he might return to his quiet little study habits.

He glanced around the plush cabin and saw that Keene had disappeared, probably gone back up to flirt with Irwin. The pilot struck Briggs as distinctly uninterested in male company, but Keene's intellect didn't exactly parallel his size. As long as he didn't interfere with her flying . . .

"Nirasawa, call up the psych profiles on our three

survivors and run persuasion thresholds . . . I want direct and indirect stim, relationship differentials, and method probabilities."

The guard had been standing patiently next to the cabin entrance, waiting for direction. "Right away, Mr. Briggs. Shall I report orally, or would you prefer an interjection in the files—"

Holy hell.

"Just write it up, let me know when you're finished," Briggs snapped, unable to sustain his irritation for more than a second. He was quite content with the smooth progression thus far and feeling positive about the outcome.

The Marine, she'll be the one. If it was volunteers only, I might run into trouble—but barring the deceased ''Pop'' Izzard, she's the most likely to have dealt with the material, and still be Company loyal . . .

Really, he'd already won. Everyone had their price, gain or loss; once he found hers, or the tech's or the volunteer's, it was just a matter of convincing them that he would live up to his half long enough to uncover the data.

If they were obtuse enough to believe him, they deserved what they would get.

The yautja didn't keep time the way humans did, but Noguchi knew they were close to the Hunt when the first ship docked to *Shell*. Just a few came aboard, all Blooded, but it was only the first; within hours, four more transports had paused long enough to discharge anywhere from two to seven Hunters, veterans all. It seemed that only Topknot's trainees would be first Hunting; the rest had come for pleasure, which reinforced what she'd already suspected—this was easily the biggest Hunt she'd seen, and she had to wonder if there was more than one queen populating whatever planet they'd be fighting on. For so many Hunters, the grounds would have to be seeded with hundreds.

After crying herself to sleep, Noguchi woke up unaccountably refreshed and at ease. Soon, she knew that she'd have to make some hard decisions; she chose to enjoy the mood rather than question it. She'd dressed in one of her three onboard "outfits," skimpy clothing she'd be embarrassed to wear anyplace but in the overhot Hunter environment—the bodysuit was Nylex, but still frayed after so much wear—and spent a few hours running through forms in the ship's *kehrite*, training room. Yautja days were about thirty hours long, and they slept for just over a third of that period. The two or three quiet hours that she could claim for herself—excepting the handful of night workers, of course—were often the best of her day.

A quick rinse in cold basin water, a breakfast of *s'pke*, a kind of fruit stew, and the rest of the ship was awake. Topknot didn't call for training, another clue that the Hunt was near; he and the other Blooded were cleaning and readying weapons, testing audio loops— they wouldn't need blending camo, what Noguchi had come to think of as the invisibility factor, since bugs didn't have eyes—and marking out territories on a screen map.

Left to their own devices, the novices riled themselves into a masculine lather, bragging, shoving, generally acting like young males of any species. Noguchi spent most of the morning avoiding them; she hung around the ship's docking connector in a corner of shadows, watching the visiting Hunters come aboard.

Tress and another unBlooded she hadn't thought of a name for yet had been assigned to greet the visitors, directing them to wherever they wanted to go—the mess hall, the armory, "guest" quarters. Another series of metallic *thumps* at the lock told her that a fifth (or was it sixth?) ship had docked. Noguchi had just about decided to call the unnamed yautja "Sakana," the Japanese word for "fish," when Topknot suddenly appeared at the mouth of the tunnel back to the main part of the ship. Half a dozen novices trailed behind him, their speckled chests heaving with excitement.

Loincloths only were the standard dress for the train-ees; Blooded generally wore chest harnesses as well, for which she continued to be thankful. The yautja wouldn't be aroused in any way by her nudity, but she was still human enough to feel some modesty.

Topknot and his followers lined up beside Tress and Sakana, the Leader speaking quickly, apparently wrapping up a speech he'd been at for a while. Noguchi stepped away from the dark corner, gleaning as much as she could from his postures and words. Her physical makeup made it nearly impossible to speak an entire sentence in their language, but after a year of total immersion, she understood a lot more than they suspected.

. . . he is—a Blooded of songs, a yautja who—wins? wins many children, has trophies of all and many enemies . . .

The Leader's respectful tone and the eagerness of his students was impressive; she'd never seen Topknot acknowledge another Hunter as anything better than competent. Whoever was docking had quite a reputation, and she decided to stay for his grand entrance.

Broken Tusk—Dachande—was sung about, all great Leaders are. Perhaps this one is actually as worthy as he was . . .

As the air lock hummed into motion, Topknot finally noticed her. He silenced the hissing young males, ignoring her. Noguchi was well aware that her presence often complicated matters; she hung back but didn't leave, determined to exercise the rights of a Blooded Hunter, doing as she pleased when not on a Hunt.

She was surprised when he stepped into view, flanked by two others. He was in front, there was no doubt who was the Leader, but he was *young*. The new arrival wore body armor but no mask; the scars across his speckled brow and on his clawed hands were extensive, but from the condition of his tusks and talons, he looked no older than an unBlooded.

Topknot greeted him, touching his shoulder and tilting his head, calling him by name, a phlegmy rattle. When the young warrior returned the gesture, Noguchi saw the piece of cloth wrapped around his wrist—

—and her vision tunneled, her heart skipping a beat. Without thinking, without making the appropriate request to approach, she stepped forward to see it better, certain that she must be mistaken.

No, can't be—

It was part of a Marine Corps banner, the three red stripes for land, sea, and aerospace, the design unmistakable—the *meaning* unmistakable, worn around his right forearm as a trophy, and she reached out to touch it—

—and remembered herself even as he backhanded her, knocking her to the floor, her arm going numb from the powerful smack.

Noguchi submitted automatically, her mind simultaneously chiding her for her stupidity and trying to rationalize the banner. The youthful Hunter stared at her for a moment along with Topknot and the others, silent and still—and then turned away, not acknowledging her apology but not interested in pursuing the matter, either. As one, the group started out of the lock, her insubordination ignored but not forgotten, Topknot already telling the newcomers about the territorial stakes.

Alone, Noguchi stayed on the floor, feeling conflicted, angry and embarrassed and horribly confused. No Hunter would wear such a thing unless, unless he'd *taken* it.

But the code, it had to have been a fair fight, the Marine must have attacked first because they won't Hunt intelligent species . . .

She couldn't even pretend to accept that. The predatory race Hunting humans? The difference in technology, in strength, in pure aggressive capacity—"fair" didn't enter into it, a Hunter could easily slip away from a human assault. It wasn't supposed to happen, there were rules against it in spite of the Clan's general xenophobia—

—and they respect him. If it's such a taboo why do they respect him? What was his punishment?

There was no point in trying to convince herself that the Hunter had suffered for his actions, and even if the Marine *had* attacked first, even if the warrior couldn't get away and was forced to kill—*she* was human.

Human, and living with a race that is disgusted by me and those like me. Hunting with a race that exalts a human killer.

This Hunt would be her last. No one would be sorry to see her go, Topknot would surely be thrilled to drop her off somewhere populated by her own kind.

And then what? Go back to corporate hustling, to a life with no life, to fifty hours a week behind a desk and no one to talk to. For excitement you could take up sport hunting, weekends spent at a sim range, firing light at a screen—and inside, the part of you that is warrior will wither and fade, and you'll be one among billions, a lonely woman marking time until she runs out of will. Your Blooding will mean nothing, it will be an ugly scar from a life you once had. No more Hunting, Machiko. How honorable you'll be . . .

Noguchi sat on the floor for a very long time, feeling things that she thought she'd left far behind.

11

The drop into Bunda's atmosphere wasn't easy, but the small shuttle's design had been loosely based on the USCMC UD-4 series—not close enough to allow for maneuverability or comfort, but Lara was willing to settle for what it *did* offer—the capacity to drop into a planet's atmosphere without burning to a crisp.

Thanks to an auto program loaded up by one of the pilots on Bunda, the shuttle broke through only moments from the survey station and flew itself to the designated coordinates, giving the three passengers an opportunity to see the world that had found them. H/K MAX teams usually stayed out in the field for months at a time, with occasional R&R stops at satellite stations—but even without weeks upon weeks of sterility to compare it to, Lara thought that she'd never seen such a beautiful place. Bunda was fantastically, wildly alive, the pale lemony sky strewn with flocks of indigenous birds, the surface thick with plants in multiple shades of green. Ellis pointed out some movement through one of the clearings they passed over, and they

saw a group of brown-furred humanoid creatures lop-
ing through the heavy grasses, tailed, each no more
than a meter high. Like primates, if Lara remembered
her history, test monkeys. Seeing them running free
through the warm, living jungle was amazing, an anti-
dote to the slaughterhouse that had been DS 949.

The three of them sat in the warming cockpit, Ellis
and Jess half-sitting on the copilot seat together. Lara
was the only one with any flying experience, although
hers was almost exclusively zero gee. It struck her
again how incredibly lucky they were; saved, with only
a few hours of air left, by people who had the technology to see them safely to this paradise.

If only it wasn't Company . . .

"There it is," Jess said, pointing roughly northeast
from their moving position. Almost as he said it, the
shuttle veered toward the station, giving them a clear
view of where they were going. It wasn't as beautiful as
Bunda, but it was close.

It was a design that Lara had heard about but never
seen—an ME.Hess, Multi-Envelope, named after the
architect who'd drafted the first, on Earth. The MEs
were relatively inexpensive, durable, and because their
contact with the ground was limited to a small number
of relatively slender stabilizing posts and a single indus-
trial lift, there was little danger of unexpected interaction with a planet's natural inhabitants—an important
consideration in unexplored environments.

"It looks like a bunch of balloons with a couple of
ledges tacked on," Jess said, and Lara smiled, nodding.
In essence, that was exactly what they were looking at;
the gigantic off-white spheres were filled with buoyant
gasses, supporting a series of decks for landing and observation, laboratories, and a decently sized living area.
The uninflated "balloons" were much cheaper to
transport than powdered plasticrete.

*And Lord knows the Company's always looking at the
bottom line—*

A rather tense male voice spoke clearly through the

'com, startling her a little. She wasn't used to being addressed by her title anymore.

"Lieutenant Lara, this is Kevin Vincent, ASM for Bunda survey, do you read?"

Acting or Active Station Manager. Lara took a deep breath and tapped the return, aware that Jess and Ellis were both watching her nervously. She'd been second-in-command for the H/K team, only Pop outranking her; for a while, at least, she'd be speaking for all of them.

"Affirmative, Mr. Vincent. This is Second Lieutenant Katherine Lara from W-Y49392 *Nemesis*. Also present are Martin Jess and Brian Ellis from *Nemesis*. On behalf of all of us, I'd like to—"

She'd wanted to thank him first thing, boost their chances for a warm reception, but Vincent cut her off.

"You'll be landing on Deck Seven, ETA four minutes. Please remain aboard until we've had a chance to verify your status; we'll let you know when you've been cleared."

Lara frowned, her gut sinking. "Mr. Vincent, I can assure you that—"

"Over and out," he said. The 'com went dead.

Ellis looked pale. "What does that mean?" he asked. "Are they—do we have to wait until they call one of the home offices? Find out who we are?"

"It means they already have," Jess said, his voice tight with anger. He glared out at the growing station, his upper lip curled. "They don't want us wandering around, telling people what really happened. Probably gonna feed us some bullshit line about quarantine."

"But it's standard protocol, isn't it?" Ellis asked. "Us coming from an infected area?"

Jess laughed, a humorless bark. "Yeah, right. We don't have sleep capacity, they'd know that. For Chrissake, if one of us was dorked and corked, we'd all be wiped by now."

They fell into an uneasy silence as the shuttle lowered itself over LZ Seven, the station giant now that they were so close, Lara keeping her hands on the controls in case the program glitched. Jess was right, Bunda wasn't worried about infection—which could only mean that someone, Grigson maybe, had sent word. They were the sole survivors from an infested DS terminal, the only witnesses to a terrible mistake made by Weyland/Yutani, and there was no way the Company was going to let them walk. What was the old saying? Out of the frying pan, into the fire . . .

As soon as the shuttle touched down, Jess stood and walked to the side hatch, talking back over his shoulder.

"We can't get off, but they didn't say anything about opening the door, did they?"

Before Lara or Ellis could move, Jess had hit the lock panel, jabbing at the controls determinedly. The thick metal door raised with a hiss and warm air flooded in, warm and almost overwhelmingly fragrant. It smelled of soil and vegetation, of sun-warmed life, of jungle rot. It was exquisite, and Lara and Ellis both stood and moved toward the open hatch, Lara feeling a reflexive need to breathe it in. She didn't notice that Jess had frozen, gazing out into the sunny morning with a look of disgust on his unshaven face.

"I guess they really don't want us to get off," he said softly.

Lara and Ellis stood on either side of him, looking at the six men and women standing some ten meters away, standing near a fuel hatch. Their expressions were grim, their bodies tensed—their hands white-knuckled on the carbine rifles they held, pointed at the open door of the shuttle.

At us.

The half dozen "guards" didn't move, didn't speak; they didn't have to. She and Jess and Ellis were prisoners, and would be until the Company decided what was to be done with them. And in that second, realizing that the situation was only going to get worse, an idea that had been gradually forming in Lara's tired mind finally took shape. It was so obvious that she could hardly believe it hadn't already occurred to her.

"Jess, Ellis. Back away from the door, slowly. We have to talk."

The *Trader*'s log had been destroyed, along with the *Trader*, the space station, their ship—but the Company didn't know that. If they did, she and the boys would be dead already.

And as long as they think we might have something they want . . .

Slowly, hands raised, the three of them moved away from the hatch, away from the light, the hope that Lara had felt at the sight of the beautiful world reborn as the idea solidified, the details falling into place.

If they played it right, there was a chance that they could walk away, after all.

Noguchi was in her quarters, sitting on her rumpled bed and lost in thought. The Hunt would begin soon, probably as soon as dusk fell over the planet *Shell* was orbiting. Most of the eggs would have hatched by now, the face-hugging embryo carriers finding incubators, the aliens born in crunches of blood and bone. They were much more active at night, on worlds that had night; most Hunts started when the day star set over the seeded planet. Even now, as the bugs began their violent domination of their new home, the Hunters would be arguing over the best sites, working through the rankings for each group of warriors, and planning path direction; Hunts usually started scattered, but almost always ended with all of the groups meeting at a predesignated site—the better to display their bloody trophies, to count losses, and step up in caste.

The problem was, she didn't know if she could Hunt this time. Seeing the human trophy carried by the young Leader had shaken her, thrown her off-balance in a way that she hadn't expected. How would she be able to find the focus she'd need to Hunt? The damage that had been done to her respect for the yautja was deep, and probably irreparable. She was afraid to leave, to go back to a way of life she didn't really understand— but she couldn't stay, either. The only question was, would she Hunt this last time? Could she?

So heavy was her introspection, the *thud* at her door made her jump. It had to be Topknot, no one else had ever come to her quarters. Noguchi stood and walked to the door, not sure what she would say to him about her behavior in the ship dock. He hadn't Blooded her, but she was still a Hunter on his ship; her actions could affect his standing among other Leaders.

To her surprise, Topknot didn't seem angry when she opened the door. He greeted her instead, his massive claw covering her shoulder, his upper and lower mandibles at rest. The Leader motioned her out of her room and toward the main part of the ship, his small eyes shaded in the low light by the thick bowl of his skull.

She stepped out into the corridor with him, somehow knowing what was next as they moved away from her room.

I've known for some time, haven't I? That it would come down to this . . .

The Leader signed as he walked, punctuating the simple gestures with simple words. He raised his hands, extending his claws. Touched his Blooding mark, a cross shape. Tapped his chest and motioned toward hers, clattering the sounds of proverb.

Those without honor are not part of the Hunt/Clan. Those who do not fight for their honor have no honor.

Noguchi signaled, fist to brow. *I know this.*

Topknot didn't speak for a moment, giving her time to prepare for the inevitable. She'd had the impression from the beginning that there was no love lost between Broken Tusk and Topknot, but he'd given her a chance, at least. For that, she still respected the Leader, even as she felt her anger rise.

The first thing she'd learned about Hunter culture was that you were only as good as your last fight; in that way, every yautja was equal, Leader and novice alike. When a Hunter's courage or honor was in doubt, he had to fight. She waited, again, already knowing.

Topknot raised his claws again, gurgling the name of her opponent.

Noguchi signaled her understanding. Shorty. She was to fight an unBlooded. If she won, her status would remain unchanged. If she lost—if any Blooded Hunter lost to a novice—

I lose my place in the Hunt. In all Hunts. In time, she'd be given a chance to prove herself again—but considering what she'd been thinking and feeling lately, there wasn't going to be a later. Her break with the Hunters was imminent.

Noguchi turned her face to an invisible sun, tracing her hand in a half circle. *When?*

"H'ka-se," Topknot growled. *Now.*

They were already walking toward the *kehrite*, the room where novices learned unarmed and simple blade combat. Noguchi took a deep breath, nodding inwardly, resigned to whatever fate lay ahead.

Win or lose, it would be a relief.

12

"**S**tupid damn gun—"

Davis Pratt jerked at the shotgun's cartridge holder as he stumbled through the bushes, wishing that he knew what the hell he was doing, or better yet, that he wasn't in the middle of the damn jungle with Rembert. Of all the men to be teamed with, something just *had* to go wrong when he was out taking samples with Harold Rembert—

"Wait, wait a second," Rembert gasped from behind him, and when Pratt felt the touch on his shoulder, he very nearly turned and shot the fat geologist.

Jesus, he's trying to give me a heart attack!

"Rembert, keep your damn hands offa me!" Pratt could hear the panic in his own voice and it only made him angrier and more afraid. He'd never seen a bug before, eleven years doing soil tests for the Company and he'd seen a video, but that was all—

—and that was one of 'em, had to be, and what the hell is it doing on Bunda?

"I don't, don't think it's, still coming," Rembert wheezed, and Pratt stopped, turning to look at the jungle that had closed up behind them. Leaves, grasses, branches, and ferns, the early-afternoon sun playing across the seemingly solid mass of green. No tall, shining darkness, no rounded, phallic skull or drooling teeth, no claws. Maybe Rembert was right.

"I think we lost it," Rembert said, his jowly young face flushed and dripping with sweat. He bent over, hands on his knees, gulping air in ragged lungfuls.

"We gotta get back to the station," Pratt said, somewhat winded himself. He wasn't in as rotten shape as Rembert, but he also wasn't a young man anymore. "Gotta report this."

Rembert didn't answer, working too hard to breathe. Pratt held up the shotgun, a heavy old thing that he'd carried for six months on Bunda and never fired before today, before twenty minutes ago. He pumped it, the satisfying *ca-chuk* of the deadly weapon making him feel only slightly less terrified. It seemed to be working now, it was stuck before, after he'd fired at the thing that had burst into the clearing where they'd stopped for lunch, no reason to think that a damn monster was going to jump out of the bushes like grinning death and—

STOP!

Pratt took a deep breath, nodding to himself, the sweat running hot down the back of his neck. Couldn't panic. Had to keep it together. Back to the station, two and a half klicks was all, tell Vincent, load everyone up on the 'copters. They only had two passenger ships capable of spaceflight, but each one held twenty; it wouldn't even be too crowded and they'd be safe. They could just orbit, wait for the Company to send an H/K team, people trained to fight the bugs, to keep them from spreading, and—

"That was an XT, wasn't it?" Rembert breathed. "One of those bugs, like in the manual."

Pratt felt another surge of anger. Harold Rembert, fat and useless and as dense as mercury. "Yeah, and we could be calling in help right now if you'd grabbed the damn radio!''

Rembert straightened up, his chins trembling. "The *radio*? I was busy ducking, you fired three times and didn't come close to hitting anything but *me*!''

Pratt wanted to punch him, right in his fat face. So he wasn't a crack marksman, he checked dirt for acidity, for hell's sake; if he'd ever suspected that he'd be running through a stinking jungle with a bug on his ass, he would have practiced more.

"I won't miss next time," he snapped, "and you still could've remembered the radio.''

Rembert didn't answer, his round face suddenly still, his eyes wide. He held up one bloated hand—

—and *crash* through the leaves, in front of them, the thing leapt out into the open, shrieking, not five meters away—

—and Rembert screamed, and ran. Pratt jerked the shotgun up, *take THAT you—*

Boom!

The blast made a huge hole through the leafy branch of a banyar tree, a full meter to the right of the creature. It reached out, its impossibly long and skeletal arm tipped with razor claws—

—and jerked the shotgun out of his hands, hissing, its spiny tail whipping through the grasses at its feet.

Fuck!

Pratt turned and sprinted away, his balls crawling into his lower belly, his sweat turning sick and cold. He ran, not hearing if the monster was behind him, not about to look, charging into the trail of still-moving leaves where the geologist had gone. The world turned into a green and sunny blur, flashing past like some terrible dream.

"*Rembert!*" He screamed, sorry for every crummy thing he'd ever thought about him, wanting nothing more than not to die alone, *please, not that—*

—and *there*, kneeling next to a native tree, hunched over, his back to Pratt.

Thank you! "Rembert, we can't stop, come on get up—"

Rembert didn't move but Pratt would make him, drag him if he had to. He tripped to a stop and grabbed Rembert's fleshy shoulder, pulling—

—and Harold Rembert fell backwards, but it wasn't the geologist, couldn't be, this man had no face, only a smooth, strange mask.

Bugs, baby bug things, no no no no—

The thought became screams but he didn't realize it, too horrified by what he was seeing.

"No no no no—"

It was a giant, pulsing, spidery crab, its thickly corded tail wrapped around the fat man's throat. It was impregnating him, that was what they did, it was how they killed, and knowing what it was doing was enough that something in his mind gave way. He didn't hear himself cry out because too much of his awareness was taken up by the terrible, terrible thing in front of him.

Pratt was still screaming when he saw the other one skittering across the fertile ground, almost too fast to see. Still screaming as it coiled its prehensile tail against the dirt and lunged at him, slick, muscular fingers sliding into his hair, a soft, wet proboscis plugging his still-screaming mouth.

Davis Pratt stopped screaming. Out loud, anyway.

13

Not everyone on *Shell* was jammed into the sticky-hot training room but it was very close. At least sixty Hunters were gathered around the slightly raised "stage," the musk of their combined aggression so thick that Noguchi could almost taste it as she and Topknot stepped into the room. The large gathering was talking loudly, laughing and pushing at each other until they saw her, at which point their clatter raised to a dull roar. It wasn't hard to inspire bloodlust in a yautja, and she had the feeling that some of them, at least, had been waiting a long time for this.

Shorty was already on the platform, dressed in a loincloth, talking excitedly to a small group of his peers. It seemed that being chosen to fight the ooman had raised his status somewhat, the other novices finally interested in what he had to say about how ugly she was, how he would crush her honor, how this was really no fight at all.

We'll just see about that . . .

Shorty fell silent as she and the Leader approached the stage, but she could see the hatred in him as easily as if he'd screamed for her blood. Already his hands were clenched, his tusks opened wide, exposing his small, toothy pink mouth.

Topknot stepped onto the platform and called for one of his Blooded to bring a mask to him, motioning for Noguchi to wait. As soon as he spoke, the Hunters fell quiet, only shuffling bodies and low trills; she barely heard them over the beating of her heart. She wasn't afraid, but knowing that her fight with Shorty would have everyone's full attention made her distinctly self-conscious.

Don't think about it, don't think about any of it. Trust in yourself, in the skills you've worked so hard to achieve and maintain.

The Blooded Hunter handed the mask to Topknot, who then handed it to her. He didn't speak a single word of encouragement or even look at her, but she was deeply moved by the gesture nonetheless. Compared to a yautja skull, hers was thin as paper.

He knows that I don't deserve this, not with a novice. She'd been Blooded when she joined them, she'd never had to prove her status in hand-to-hand, and being asked to fight an unBlooded was a serious slight. Hunter politics that she couldn't begin to understand were at play here, perhaps instigated by the young Leader she'd dared to touch.

Topknot spoke and gestured as she donned the mask, his deep, rolling voice filling the heated air. Noguchi only half translated to herself, too intent on her breathing, on psyching herself up for the fight.

. . . this is Clan and not Clan waging for honor . . . standard rules . . . when the matter is decided the first transports will leave for Hunt . . .

Deep breaths, slow and even. Her ragged braids were already plastered to her skull, her face dripping in the close confines of the mask. She heard Shorty's name and then her own, the name bestowed on her by Broken Tusk, Dahdtoudi.

Small knife, it means small knife because I am small but

*deadly sharp, and I will win. I will best my opponent because
I am faster and sharper, I am a warrior and he is no one.*
Standard rules, whoever was knocked off the stage or
knocked out first lost the fight. Shorty would lose, *I am
the better fighter, more experienced* . . .

The crowd roared anew as Topknot stepped off the
lightly padded platform and Shorty moved to the corner farthest from her. It was time. Noguchi closed her
eyes for a half second, found her center, then boosted
herself onto the stage with one hand.

As soon as she was on her feet, Shorty crouched,
growling, his arms spread wide. He was small for a
Hunter but bigger than she, probably twice her weight
if only a half meter taller. If he managed to get his
claws on her, the fight would be over.

So don't let it happen.

It was the last full thought she had before she let
her instincts take over, crouching herself, ready to de-
fend. The yautja howled for action, the platform trembling as they crushed against it for a better view.

With a wild, guttural scream, Shorty rushed her.
He thrust one meaty hand forward to swat at her head,
easily enough power to break her neck—

—and she sidestepped as she reached up and
cupped his wrist with both of her hands, swung her upper body into his lunge, down and left. She let him do
the work, simply redirecting his charge.

Wham! Shorty went down, landing heavily on one
shoulder, his weight pulling him ass over to land flat on
his back. The room erupted in excited shouts, fury and
disbelief and a desire for more, more battle, blood or
death.

The unBlooded yautja crawled to his feet, his mandibles spreading wide as he screamed his anger. He was
furious, *use it*—

A leap toward her and Shorty swept his right arm
at her head, still shrieking. Noguchi dropped, bringing
her leg out and around, hitting the hot flesh of his an-
kles with the side of her foot as hard as she could.

Wham!

As soon as he hit the floor she was up, dancing backwards, barely hearing the cacophony of almost feral screams that filled the *kehrite*.

Shorty lunged up from where he'd fallen, the hatred in his tiny eyes now tainted with something new, pain, uncertainty, she didn't bother to guess. He *flew* at her, kicking off from the padded floor, his entire body a ram that would crush her—

—and she kicked her feet up and out, landed on her butt as he reached her, lifted her legs and found his muscled belly with her bare feet. A single motion, Shorty continued his limited flight over her rolling body as she helped him along.

Wham, and there was a grunt of escaping air this time, a sound of pain and shock that only she could hear over the shrill cries of the watchers.

—finish this—

She leapt up and took one running jump, Shorty still rising from the stage, *side of the knee—*

—and her right foot slammed into his leg, not breaking the cap but surely bruising it badly, definitely pain on his face now as he reflexively grabbed his wound—

—and Noguchi landed and spun, bringing her foot up again, the full force of her body's momentum behind the roundhouse kick to his jaw. Strings of saliva flew from his mouth and he collapsed, elbows on the floor, his head hanging.

On all fours as he was, there was little chance that she could knock him off of the platform—but rendering him unconscious was a distinct possibility, and definitely the more gratifying of the two. She couldn't let him recover, it would have to be fast, and she stepped back, ready to run, to deliver another well-placed kick—

—and someone grabbed her foot. Talons closed around her ankle, holding on, pulling her off-balance.

No!

She looked over her shoulder, saw only a sea of screaming faces, but it didn't matter who, she had to get loose before Shorty regained himself.

She dropped as if to do a push-up and kicked back with her free leg. Her foot hit flesh, hard, the smooth feel of tusk against the sole telling her that she'd found her mark. The grip on her ankle fell away and she scrabbled to her feet, struggling to find her center again—

—and was slammed into, her head rocked back by the rounded dome of Shorty's skull, a head butt that knocked her backwards and made the shouts and faces and heat blur into a single thing, a noise-light that hurt—

—and before she could fall, Shorty's arms were grabbing at her, one giant fist raised, her head pushed down and she could only see the padded floor—

—and the pain was tremendous, a ton of hot metal landing across the back of her head. His fist, knocking her flat, the floor blessedly cool against her bare abdomen. Her limbs suddenly felt far away and she knew that if he hit her again, he would probably kill her. In the space of only a few seconds, the fight had turned, turned and cemented an outcome.

Noguchi saw the clawed foot in front of her, saw it pull back, saw her only chance; with what little coordination she could muster, she raised herself, hands and knees, tightening her gut—

—and when he kicked her, the top of his foot connecting solid with her tensed muscles, she let it carry her. She flew, screams rising up, enveloping her moving form, hot musk filling her senses—

—and she hit the floor, skidding, tall bodies moving aside to let her flesh finally stop her. Dazed and in pain, she lay on her back, catching her breath, trying to catalog her injuries as sixty or more Hunters roared their approval. Shorty's voice seemed loudest of all, a wordless shriek of triumph that hurt even worse than her head.

She'd fought honorably, and lost because they
hated her, because they couldn't stand to see her suc-
ceed. Who would believe her, who would say that
they'd witnessed the cheat?

Doesn't matter . . .

She closed her eyes behind the stifling mask, making no move to rise, not sure if she was angry or sad or
relieved. She was alive, and no one could brand her a
coward—but she'd lost her place in the Hunt.

No one reached down to help her to her feet, and
that felt like the answer she'd been waiting for. After a
year, it was finally over.

14

The sounds that poured up from the jungle as a pale twilight fell over Bunda were soothing, making Ellis feel sleepy in spite of their circumstances. They were Earth sounds, some of them, gently repetitive insect noises that reminded him of a childhood long dead. He'd been sleeping too much, he knew, but his body was still recovering from the interface; he couldn't help feeling tired.

Seven hours thirteen minutes and still aboard the shuttle, no contact at all with the people living on the station despite Lara's repeated efforts. Jess had even tried to engage a couple of the guards, but they weren't interested. Either they really believed that there was a risk of alien infection or they had been ordered not to talk to them.

Ellis sat cross-legged in the back of the shuttle, Max towering over him, hunched and empty. Lara and Jess were still in the cockpit, trying to raise Mr. Vincent from the station. Their voices seemed distant. Ellis figured it was because the hatch was still open; the cooling Bunda air had a life of its own, a rich presence that filled the shuttle and separated the occupants with its thickness . . .

. . . *more crazy thinking, maybe, but we don't care, do we?*

Max said nothing. Of course, it wasn't alive, had never been alive even when its guts had been human. Ellis only had to close his eyes to see the dead volunteer he'd pulled out of the machine back on DS 949, the insanity written in cruel lines across his pain-wracked face, his emaciated frame wrapped in circuits and lines and tubes. Pop had given Ellis the order to run the full program, up to stage three—massive doses of synthetic adrenaline pumped into the volunteer, creating something even more savage than an alien horde—and it had killed him.

When Ellis had slid into Max, he'd had no idea what would happen. His only concerns at the time were the echoing screams on his headset, from Teape and Jess. Pulaski had already been dead by then, eviscerated and bled out—and when Pop's voice had coolly informed them that they were dead, that he wasn't going to be picking them up . . .

. . . *I got in. I got in, and stopped being Brian alone. I became . . . us.*

Max's huge orange body was pitted and scratched, acid spots randomly spattered across its plated chest, but it still looked as powerful and deadly as when they'd first met. Its left arm was tipped with a revolving liquid-propulsion grenade launcher and pulse rifle, its right a tri-capacity M210 flamethrower; even sitting still, it was a formidable creature. They had worked well together, Ellis's mind computer and Max's physical—awareness, if that was the right word. It was strange, how before they'd interfaced, Max had been MAX, just a machine. Ellis couldn't look at it now and think that; he'd *been* with Max, shared consciousness with it. It was just a machine the way that a diamond was just a rock.

Ellis gazed up at its soulless face, thinking about the

predicament they were in now. Lara had worked up a story about having looped the *Trader*'s log on a locked channel before the explosion; she said that it was their only chance, that they could count on being killed if they didn't stick together . . .

. . . *the way Max and I were together* . . .

Ellis smiled dreamily. He and Max couldn't join again, it would probably kill him, but the idea, the memory was a comfort. Lara and Jess had been so worried about him afterward, thinking that he wouldn't recover, but it wasn't like that. He'd recovered, he just understood more now, about what it meant not to be alone. About how dying wasn't so bad, when you'd been a part of something greater than yourself—

"What are you smiling about, kid?"

Ellis looked up at Jess and shook his head, still smiling. Jess was his friend, he was the man who'd led Max Ellis through the infestation, but he couldn't possibly understand. Lara, either. They'd think he was still . . . unwell.

"Nothing, really," he said. "Just how things change, you know?"

Jess smiled back, but Ellis could see that he was hesitant about it. "Yeah, sure. We almost die, survive, almost die, survive again."

Ellis nodded. "And now we wait for the Company to finish the story."

Jess's smile disappeared. Ellis saw the cold spark in his dark eyes, his feelings about Weyland/Yutani and what they'd done to his team an all-consuming rage. Ellis could see it as plainly as he could see that Jess was trying to fight it.

"We keep to our story, they won't do anything," Jess said slowly, as if to reassure Ellis that they would survive.

Ellis nodded again, and Jess walked stiffly away, back to where Lara was continuing her open hail. It was sad, that Jess still carried so much pain . . .

Well. That was Jess's battle, not his.

Ellis turned back to gaze at Max, remembering how they'd blasted great, smoking holes through the alien mass, how Max had saved him, how they had saved the others, 3017 rounds/121 M108 canister grenades launched 17.57 liters napthal fuel ignited within the terminal space . . .

Max was silent. Ellis sat and remembered, for both of them.

The dizziness and nausea had been the worst, the blow to her head leaving her feeling out of touch with herself and her surroundings, but after a few hours' rest, she'd recovered. The rest of the damage was minor: a twisted ankle, the back of her neck bruised, her abs as sore as if she'd performed a thousand crunches. In another day or two, she'd be good as new.

Lucky me.

Noguchi stood at the door to the nest in the empty lower dock, staring in at the captive queen, not feeling much of anything. A sadness, perhaps. The last of the transports had departed, gone for the Hunt; there were only eleven yautja still on board, shipworkers all, and the giant *Shell* felt as empty and hollow as she did.

The Hunt would go on into the early-morning hours; she'd already decided to speak to Topknot when he returned, after the Hunters' feast. Considering the nomadic nature of the Hunter culture, she had no doubts that they'd be passing a human outpost within a few weeks. She wouldn't be treated very well in the time she had left with them, but she'd fought competently enough to hold her head up. Besides, she'd gotten used to being treated poorly . . .

"But you're not, are you," she said softly, putting her hand on the window, looking at the giant, unmoving darkness strapped to the back wall. It was the first time she'd been down to see the imprisoned queen since her narrow escape from the nest, and she didn't like what she saw. There was a single shaft of puny light shining down over the trapped mother, casting most of her in deep shadow. All of her impossibly strong limbs, shackled. Her tiered, lustrous comb, chained back. And most depressing, the thick cord strung between her outer jaws, gagging her.

The queen was tightly tied, the only real movement that of the eggs sliding through the short, membranous sac that she'd created only hours after being placed; eggs that were deposited onto a weight-triggered conveyer belt and moved to the side, ready to be loaded into a remote and sent off to some distant world.

In spite of her general dislike of drama, Noguchi found herself trying to draw some analogy between herself and the queen, perhaps because looking at the trapped animal made her feel the same vague sadness she felt for herself. They were both female. Both out of their element. Hindered warriors, maybe. Beaten down by the Hunters, surely . . .

. . . but not anymore, not for me.

She couldn't watch any longer, it was like watching an insect impaled on a pin, dying slowly. Noguchi turned away, walking carefully toward the lift that would carry her back to the main rooms.

Past empty shelves, past an empty hallway, through the gate to the elevator platform. She touched the symbol of the clawed hand on the control panel and the machine hummed to life, rising smoothly, dark walls sliding past.

The thought of seeing, speaking to people again, was a frightening one—but exciting, too. What would she say, to explain where she'd come from? Telling the truth, she ran the risk of being whisked away to some corporate debriefing that could last months, depending on who owned the outpost. Chigusa was probably safe, they were an agribusiness. But Weyland/Yutani, or Biotech . . . it was common knowledge that they were always looking for weapon apps and didn't mind exploiting whatever or whoever could bring them new opportunities.

Noguchi grinned as the elevator pulled to a stop, thinking about what a stir it would cause if she handed a burner over to the corporate community. Or a suit of armor, fully loaded—wrist blades, sound loop, filter system, and infra eyes . . .

She stepped off the lift, still smiling—and realized that she *was* smiling. Not about her performance as a fighter, or for shaming a novice, or because she remembered something that had made her laugh from a long time before. She was smiling because she was Machiko Dahdtoudi Noguchi, and she was getting the fuck away from the fucking Hunters, and how hard could having a conversation about work or the weather be, after the year she'd had?

The burst of giddy good humor lasted as long as it took her to limp two steps away from the elevator. The *Shell* was not her home, but Earth hadn't been her home, either. Her entire life prior to her meeting with Broken Tusk had been a pallid one. Socially, living with the Clan had been terrible—but the Hunt itself . . .

Nothing matched the thrill of risking everything against success. On Earth, people paid small fortunes to experience even a taste of the hyperawareness and adrenaline high that came from putting one's life on the line, and that was only a taste. It was simulation, a fake; there was always an out, a panic button, no matter what the experience, the liability laws firmly established.

Suddenly, she felt a deep longing for what was happening on the planet below the cloaked *Shell*, the screams of triumph, the hot reek of pouring acid-splash, the dance with the blade. The Hunt, that she'd never know again, and not because she'd chosen to turn away. She'd been cheated, systematically worn down and forced out, it wasn't fair and she hated them for taking her very life from her.

Noguchi limped slowly to her quarters, wanting nothing more than to sleep for a while.

15

Kelly Irwin was pleasantly surprised to hear a familiar voice coming up from Bunda, particularly after taking orders from Dickhead Briggs for the last couple of weeks—not to mention fending off his man Keene, the walking steroid. It was enough to make a girl want to get shit-faced drunk, and her only hope for Bunda was that the science boys had a stash of something or other put aside for emergencies.

She'd sent a standard comp alert to the station and had already dropped the lux Sun Jumper into the upper reaches, the planet a dark blur beneath them, before she made vocal contact. The necessary info had been shot back and forth and triple-checked via the Herriman-Weston FC, but Irwin liked the personal touch, always had. Sun Jumpers were so state that she was bored, the auto self-monitoring and IFTDS making it about as complicated to fly as a paper plane.

Stifling a yawn, Irwin put in the call, watching the fly-by-light with only half an eye.

"Bunda survey, this is WY-1117 requesting confirmation of landing clearance, come back." The planet looked pretty in the early starlight, at least, lots of greenery. She was a city girl herself, but nature made a nice backdrop.

"WY-1117, you're cleared for Three . . . Irwin, is that you?"

She grinned, suddenly awake. She recognized Matt Windy's soft tones, the clipped way he said her name. He'd been training in communications and pattern control at the same WY program she'd gotten her license from, Earthside. *Buddha, how long's it been? Six, seven years?*

"I'll be dipped! Windy, I didn't know you was working the outskirts. What'd you do, piss in some-one's drink?"

He laughed. "Hey, Company pays top to anyone willing to leave the known universe, don't knock it. What's your excuse?"

"Playing chauffeur, thanks *so* much for reminding me. Anyway, gets me off of the merch runs, nice change of pace," Irwin said. "At least usually . . ."

Windy laughed again. "Usually? Don't tell me you're not enjoying a *Jumper*, that's some kind of pilot sacrilege, isn't it?"

Irwin grinned again. "Actually, I *am* getting bored, but it's more the suit, this time. Briggs, Lucas. A real tight-ass. He's been after me to bend the laws of physics since Zen's Respite—and *no*, I was not allowed to enjoy any of the Company amenities, so shut the fuck up."

When Windy spoke again, some of the humor had bled from his voice. "Hey . . . you know what all this is about? The Assman won't—"

Irwin interrupted, smiling. "Assman?"

"ASM, you twit. Vincent."

Cute, she hadn't heard that one. "Anyway, you were saying?"

Windy pitched his voice even lower. "He won't tell us what's going on. Shuttle lands this A.M., he says it comes from XT, but no way they've got chambers on that thing, and the heads up we got says it happened days ago. So they can't be carrying, right?"

Irwin glanced at the cabin screen before she answered. Everyone was still belted, though Briggs looked constipated as usual, shifting in his seat. Whoever was on that shuttle, he wanted 'em *bad*.

"Got me," she said quietly. "Don't ask, don't tell, you know? It's big, though. This guy's hooked up, had the full service at Zen, priority calls on scramble, two hunks of meat in suits following him to the head, with wipes. And keep shut on this, but we left Zen's Respite yesterday, dig? Before your ASM put in the call. You wanna make some points, tell him to get his ass out on that deck."

"He's been out there for the last twenty minutes, since your comp signal," Windy said. "Assman's sweating on this, and I don't blame him."

While they were talking, the Sun Jumper had dropped to an LZ alt, the dark treetops spinning beneath them like a corrugated sea. At the edge of her vision, Irwin thought she saw a flash of light somewhere deep in the jungle. It was gone before she could finish turning her head, but it reminded her that she wasn't getting paid to actually enjoy herself. Time to pay attention.

"Listen, gotta fly," she said. "You still gonna be on channels after we land?"

"Affirmative."

"Meet you in ten, then," she said, and tapped off the 'com, calling up a list of stats in the same movement. Fan pressure, skis down, bleed flaps flux, the numbers as text as they got. A yawn. Good ol' Windy, though. Briggs could go play corporate cloak and dagger; she was going to find Windy and see if he still had a taste for cheap whiskey, among other things.

Of all the outposts in the known goddamn universe they pick mine to land on, as if I didn't have enough to do already, bringing the Company down on the back of my goddamn neck—

"Do you hear something?"

Kevin Vincent glanced at Cabot, then turned his face back to the star-flecked sky, uninterested in hearing anything unless it was Briggs's ship. "No."

Cabot persisted. "I thought I heard . . . like a howl or something."

Probably Rembert, howling for supper.

To say so would be cruel; Cabot and the missing geologist were friends. Pratt and Rembert hadn't checked in since before lunch, and day teams were required to put a call in every eight hours, which meant they were officially a couple hours overdue. No big deal, except they wouldn't answer a 26 hail, the code for, "drop everything and answer your goddamn radio."

Vincent rubbed the back of his neck, sighing. They'd probably just dropped their damn radio, but it was one more hassle in a day of hassles. He'd have to send out a team if they hadn't shown by midnight. With any luck at all, Briggs would have his business finished by then and be gone.

Sure, why would he want to stay here? Little operation like this, no frills, he'll want to be out of here before the dust settles—

His wishful thinking was interrupted when he heard what Cabot had. A distant sound, southwest of the station maybe a couple of klicks—a kind of weird, harsh trilling sound, like nothing he'd ever heard before. Cabot looked at him, a vaguely smug expression in his eyes.

"Mating season?" Vincent asked, knowing that it wasn't. And he'd never heard a sound like that coming out of a primacet, the only Bunda inhabitant with lungs big enough to project that kind of noise . . .

Before Cabot could do more than shake his head, the lights of a transport ship appeared on the near horizon, followed closely by the rumbling purr of an expensive engine. To hell with strange noises, probably an injured bird. Vincent had more important things to deal with.

He straightened his shoulders as the small ship moved toward them, wishing he'd never agreed to the admin position. He'd been six months away from his phytobiology doctorate when his theory on the medical applications of bryophytes had crashed and burned. The Bunda position was only two years and the idea of being an ASM had been appealing, a chance to raise his income, to relax far away from the viciously fevered world of scientific patenting . . .

. . . and what I got was a shitload of paperwork and the nickname "Assman." And the joy of groveling before men like Briggs.

The ship was a Sun Jumper, a private-elite. Briggs was definitely the highest suit ever to come to Bunda, the ship worth more than Vincent would see in his lifetime, with extensions. It smoothly moved over the deck, the blast of heated air from its thrusters whipping at their clothes, and set down as gently as an extremely expensive feather.

Before the engines had finished powering down, a ramp slid out from near the back of the ship and the shining metal above it parted, melting to either side. Vincent and Cabot waited, Vincent taking a deep breath, reminding himself that this would be over soon.

Lucas Briggs stepped out onto the ramp looking as cool and elegant as he'd looked over the 'phone, his impeccably tailored suit the color of dried blood. Two men—two very large men—stepped out behind him, their stone faces and darting gazes telling Vincent who they were. Keene was the blond who'd placed the call on Briggs's behalf; the other was of some Asian descent that Vincent couldn't place. Both looked extremely capable.

Vincent cleared his throat and stepped forward, determined to make things pleasant. "Welcome to Bunda,

Mr. Briggs. This is Tom Cabot, our Research Team Co-ordinator. I hope that you had—"

"Save the pleasantries, Vincent," Briggs said, step-ping close enough that Vincent could smell his subtle cologne. He had that lightly tanned, muscle-stim look that the privileged tended to wear to parties, and an at-titude to match. If he noticed Cabot at all, he didn't bother acknowledging him, and hardly glanced at Vin-cent's face.

"Where are they?" Briggs asked, apparently not in-terested in extending any pleasantries himself.

Terrific. "Deck Seven, sir. As requested, they've been isolated and watched since their arrival . . ."

Briggs didn't seem to be too big on expressing praise, either. Vincent continued, feeling entirely out of his league.

". . . and, I'm sure you're eager to—ah, interview them. If you'll follow me . . . ?"

Briggs looked bored. "Nirasawa, Keene, go with him, search the shuttle. I'll be along shortly, I want to make sure Irwin refuels before she goes wandering off."

The bastard was addressing his own people, ignor-ing him entirely. Vincent gritted his teeth in what he hoped looked like a smile, saw Cabot assume the care-fully blank expression of a man on the brink of rolling his eyes.

Lord, please keep this man from ruining my life . . .

Briggs was waiting.

"Of course," Vincent said, motioning toward the deck's flight prep room behind them; he'd had it cleaned for Briggs's arrival, although he was starting to see that trying to impress Lucas Briggs would be a monumental waste of time. "Mr. Cabot, please show Mr. Briggs to Seven when he's finished his business here. This way, gentlemen."

The two blank-faced guards followed obediently as Briggs turned around and moved back up the ramp. Cabot looked miserable, but Vincent couldn't muster much sympathy for the man; if Briggs decided to fuck with them, file a report on Bunda, "Kevin Vincent" was going to be the name at the top.

Thinking of how great it was going to be when the contract expired on his administrative experience, Vincent led the guards through the efficiently bland prep room, the bizarre sound that he and Cabot had heard a few moments earlier the very last thing on his mind.

16

The shabby little transport was clean, no trace of the log in the system or on hard copy. It would have made things a lot easier, of course, but Briggs wasn't particularly disappointed. He was a negotiator, not some Company thug. Without a challenge, what was the point?

Not that there will be much challenge here . . .

He could see how easy his job would be from outside as he'd watched his guards finish their search, Vincent watching over them anxiously. The three people he'd come to see were in terrible shape, grubby and tired-looking, not to mention rather fragrant. Even outside, the warm Bunda air pressing down from a cloudless night sky, he caught the unpleasant scent of their nervous sweat and unwashed bodies . . .

. . . and that horrible musky smell . . . That seemed to be coming from the dark wilderness far below, where unseen creatures shuffled randomly through the undergrowth. He hoped his runners would cave quickly; Bunda was one of those stinking Company murkholes that wouldn't be livable until they

cleared the green, hooked up a compressor, and paved it over with plasticrete.

It shouldn't take long; the trio backed against the wall inside had the helpless look of the desperately unprepared, and would probably give up the data before he could even finish his pitch. It was anticlimactic, really.

Assume nothing. Be ready, be sincere, don't forget what's at stake.

Briggs breathed deeply, realizing that he was a little nervous himself; he tended toward overconfidence when he was uncertain. If they didn't have the log, it was all for nothing . . .

No. They had it. Positive thinking.

When Nirasawa called the shuttle empty, Briggs stepped aboard, silently reaffirming the names with the faces as he motioned his men to move back, give him some room. They did the best they could, looking strangely dwarfed by the MAX at the back wall. Vincent made no move to leave, leaning against one of the pilot seats, although his man Cabot had already disappeared. Briggs thought about asking the botanist to do the same, but decided it didn't matter; he would know better than to open his mouth—and if he didn't, or if things got out of hand, one less paper-pushing biotech was no great loss.

He smiled gently at the ragged trio, remembering the psych profiles, *open conversation to begin, see which way they're already leaning* . . .

"My name is Lucas Briggs," he said, letting the little smile fade, letting his face take on the sadness that their drama inspired. "As a Weyland/Yutani representative, please allow me to express our deepest sympathies to you for what you must have experienced on DS 949. I'm not sure if you're aware, but there's a possibility that one of our executives may have been involved in perpetuating this tragedy. I want to assure you that the matter will be thoroughly investigated."

No one spoke, although Briggs saw that they were

listening very carefully. He looked down, a touch of embarrassment in his gaze when he raised his head again.

"On a more personal note, I'd like to apologize for keeping you here all day, it's entirely my fault. I'd asked Mr. Vincent to hold you until I arrived, and there were some mechanical problems on my ship, a connection break . . . in any case, I meant to be here hours ago and was unable to send a message to tell him I was delayed. I'm truly sorry, and if you'd like to take showers or eat before we talk, stretch your legs, perhaps, I'd understand."

It was Katherine Lara who shook her head, taking the lead. "No, thank you. We're fine."

Briggs nodded, relief in his eyes, *that's what you think, you people need to bathe*, smiling a little. "Well, that's good. I won't keep you any longer than necessary."

So far, not much of a read. Lara was nervous, but obviously still the one to negotiate with. The convict, Jess, held so very still that Briggs decided he was probably struggling to hold his temper; his profile suggested anger problems. And Ellis seemed—tired, perhaps. Dazed. Briggs couldn't see his alleged injury and decided that it was probably some sort of head trauma. They were all still listening, that was the important thing; the bit about a Company exec being involved should have erased any doubts they had about his honesty, and his apology for keeping them waiting had established his sincerity.

Now, then. They're as ready as they're going to be.

Briggs clasped his hands in front of him, as if pleased and excited about what he was going to say next. Nice, not to have to fake all of it.

The suit was so full of shit, he squeaked. Jess had been a little surprised at the admission of Company involvement, but it was as carefully designed as the rest of his patronizing little act.

''Trust me, I'm your friend''—the windup, and . . . here's the pitch!

"The Company has authorized me to make retribution to you, for the terrible losses you've suffered," Briggs said, his black eyes shining as though he were about to give them some incredible gift. "Substantial retribution. Not only will you receive the *Nemesis*'s full bonus, we want to make certain that all of you feel that your futures are secure with Weyland/Yutani."

Arrogant, lying, backstabbing bastard—

"Whether or not you decide to continue with the Company, we'll see to it that your contracts are renegotiated to bring you the financial gain and freedom that you deserve, for having been the unfortunate victims in this matter. Whether or not a Company employee was involved, the incident at 949 never should have happened."

Briggs finally paused, apparently having shoveled enough for the moment. The twin muscle boys hovered in the background, arms crossed, their faces unreadable. Kevin Vincent, the asshole who'd kept them stuck on the shuttle all day, was the only one with any expression at all—and he looked mildly terrified.

Jess wanted to spit in the suit's eye, but kept his face as blank as the threatening bookends that flanked the Max; he'd promised to keep cool, Lara was calling this one and he wasn't going to blow it.

"We—appreciate this, Mr. Briggs," Lara said, "really. But all we want is to get back to Earth, try to put all this behind us."

Briggs nodded, smiling even wider, and for the first time since he'd come aboard, Jess saw the thread of steel buried beneath the layers of plastic.

Will the real Lucas Briggs, please stand up . . .

"Whatever you want. I'll make the arrangements tonight." The grin sharpened, glittering as brightly as his eyes. "Although there are a few final details that I need to get confirmation on, before we conclude our business. Specifically, there was a ship's log that was supposed to be downloaded to the *Nemesis*, from a Company transport on board the DS station. The *Trader*?"

Lara had this one nailed. He's good, but not as good as he thinks.

Lara nodded slowly. "We downloaded it."

Briggs was dancing inside, Jess could see it. He shot a glance at Ellis, but the kid didn't seem to be tuned in, he was watching the bodyguards. Or maybe the Max.

"To *Nemesis*?" Briggs asked, too quickly.

Lara shook her head. "No. Well, originally to the *Nemesis*, but there were some problems with the initial transfer, so we backed it up. I sent a locked copy to one of Pop's—Commander Izzard's—personal channels. He had a few accounts that weren't on Company file."

She smiled weakly before pushing on, a sheepish look on her face. Jess was impressed.

"I know it's not reg, but he seemed to think it was important to have a duplicate—and it *was* an order. And since the *Nemesis* was destroyed . . ."

Briggs tried to put on a look of admonishment, but couldn't quite pull it off. "You're right, it wasn't regulation. Personal transfers of Company information is not only unethical, it's illegal." A pause, a conspiratorial look that made Jess grind his teeth. "But, since you've admitted it openly and you *were* following his orders, I see no reason for any disciplinary action . . ."

He smiled, the all-forgiving suit once again. ". . . and to be honest, that log is important to Weyland/Yutani. I'm just glad it survived the, ah, tragedy."

You used that one already, Briggs, how 'bout "catastrophe," or maybe "misadventure"? Jess hated him and what he stood for, he was a liar and a front man for liars, for murderers, *keep it together, Jess, don't give in*—

Another shark's smile, and a nod to one of his guards. "So . . . account number?"

Lara met his gaze evenly. "I'd like some insurance first, Mr. Briggs. That we'll have safe passage back to

Earth. In fact, I'd like to get to Earth before we turn that information over to you."

Briggs frowned, still smiling. "Ms. Lara, you have my *word*."

That was it. Before he could stop himself, Jess opened his mouth.

"We all know what that's worth, don't we?" Jess sneered. "Come off it, we know what you're trying to cover up, so stop already with your fuckin' song and dance!"

Silence, and everyone was looking at him, and Jess was too pissed to care, the man was a goddamn *liar*, if he was going to bribe them, at least let him be up front about it, about *something*. Jess didn't give a shit if Briggs killed him, there was a redness in front of his eyes that pounded at him, heat and fury, making him clench his fists and step toward the lying murderer—

—and the resignation and sorrow on Lara's face stopped him. It wasn't just his life. Jess closed his eyes for a second, forcing the red haze away, forcing some measure of control back.

Fix it, gotta fix it—

"Jess—" Lara said, but Briggs cut her off, fixing his now not-so-warm gaze on Jess's. The guards didn't move away from the back wall, but they unfolded their arms, watching closely.

"And just what am I trying to 'cover up'?" Briggs asked.

Jess took a deep breath, exhaled it sharply. He hadn't screwed it for them, not yet, he could still salvage Lara's plan.

If I'm careful, very fucking careful.

"What the Company did to those people," he said, working his anger, watching Briggs's eyes for any hint that the suit wasn't buying it. Briggs didn't twitch one way or the other, *play it through—*

"You want the log, you're going to have to give us a little more than new contract negotiations," he snapped. "Lara and Ellis and I want to be the hell away from you before we give it up—and we're looking for bigger money than a goddamn H/K bonus."

There was another silence, long enough for Jess to realize that the impassive Briggs knew he was faking. It was over, he'd just committed suicide and dragged Lara and the kid along for the ride. His temper, his goddamn temper, *Lara, Ellis, I'm so sorry*—

Briggs grinned—then laughed, shaking his head. When he spoke again, his voice had dropped half an octave, becoming as cold and hard as only a heartless suit's could be. No more apologies, no more playing.

"All right, you've got us," he said. "Let's talk numbers."

Jess wanted to be relieved, but could still feel the rage swirling in his gut like some boiling river. And every second they were with Briggs, it was going to get harder and harder to control.

Lara felt her insides melt. Briggs had bought it, Jess had pulled it off, but it had been close. She'd known Jess long enough to know that he'd been doing some serious dancing to cover for a slip, and she wasn't going to risk letting it happen again.

As if I could stop it . . . She had to try. Ellis was getting worse; he'd been dreamily silent most of the afternoon and was now watching all of them as though he were some distant observer. They had to get him to a doc, and fuck the Company anyway. They could file charges when and if they made it home.

She cleared her throat, drawing the exec's attention back to her. "We can worry about that after you get us the hell off of this rock," she said coolly, continuing Jess's ploy. "Don't worry, we won't ask for more than we think it's worth. Now, why don't you see what you can do about a ship?"

Briggs laughed again, all pretense of sympathy and sincerity gone, and Lara felt her own anger rise up. She'd never loved the Company, but hadn't hated them, either, not until Pop had admitted his orders from Grigson. This man was laughing over the graves of hundreds.

She shot a warning glance at Jess, hoping to God that he didn't lose it again.

Briggs finally chuckled to a stop. "Of course, of course. I can't tell you how—surprised I am, I suppose you could say. I had no idea that the three of you would turn out to be . . . Company loyal."

Jess smiled, but his eyes were dangerously bright. "Are you kidding? A break like this doesn't come by every day, not for people like us."

Jess, don't, don't fuck around—

Briggs nodded. "Once in a lifetime. We've experimented before, but this was the first full-scale operation."

"Really?" Jess asked. "I would have thought—"

"Jess, I want to get out of here, get a bath," Lara interrupted, praying that she sounded casually disinterested in their conversation, praying that he'd shut the hell up. "And Ellis needs to get some rest, remember?"

"I'm okay," Ellis said, looking at Briggs as if seeing him for the first time. "What were some of the experiments?"

Fuck.

Briggs lowered his voice conversationally, leaning toward them with a smug half smile. Now that he wasn't pretending to be their favorite uncle, he'd relaxed considerably.

"I'm really not at liberty to discuss these things," he said, with the tone of a man who wanted very much to discuss them. To tell them how extremely clever he was. "I mean, you understand how important it is for the Company to maintain its edge over the competition, and what the XT means to our military applications programs . . . so let's just say that nobody would want to buy what we're selling if they didn't have the proper documentation. DS 949 was specific to how fast an infestation spreads through an isolated community, but we've also done extensive work in other arenas. I'm sure you can deduce the rest.''

Oh, God. Oh my God.

"It wasn't an accident," Jess said dully, and Lara didn't know how to stop him, didn't know if she could, her mind reeling. She felt sick, and shocked beyond simple repair.

On purpose, they did it on purpose, and sent us in to gather the results . . .

Briggs's eyes narrowed at Jess's tone, but he didn't seem to understand, not yet. "Of course it wasn't an accident. Believe me, it wasn't a decision that was made lightly, either. We had several billion dollars invested in that installation. And we did *not* tell Commander Izzard to kill you people, I hope you understand that . . .''

He trailed off, looking between the three of them, the realization dawning in his eyes.

"You don't have it, do you?" He asked.

Amazingly, it was Ellis who had the presence of mind to answer him. "Oh, we have it. And if anything happens to us—''

"You fucking bastard!"

Jess leapt for Briggs, his eyes wild, spittle flying from his lips. He grabbed the surprised exec's shoulders, still screaming, shaking him.

"They fucking DIED, they died, do you fucking understand—''

"Keene, Nirasawa!"

Jess was hauled off of the sputtering Briggs by the guards, his furious shouts cut short by a sharp, violent jab to the gut from the blond man. The Japanese grunt put one hand on Lara's shoulder, one on Ellis's, and squeezed hard enough that tears sprang to Lara's eyes. Behind them, Vincent let out a surprised squeak.

Gasping and doubled over, Jess vomited bile on the shuttle floor. Briggs stepped back, a sneer of distaste on his thin lips, straightening his suit with quick, angry fingers.

"Keene, again," Briggs said.

With a small, mean smile, the blond held on to Jess's collar, half-supporting him, Jess still trying to get his air back. Keene punched him once in the face, a hard blow to the jaw that rocked Jess's head back. Blood flew from his gasping lips.

"I will have that access code, make no mistake," Briggs spat, staring straight into Lara's wet gaze. "The only question is, how long will your friends have to suffer before you give it to me?"

17

Irwin was as drop-dead as Windy remembered, bright, casually sexy, and possessing a mouth that she probably shouldn't kiss her mother with; he liked that in a woman, femme types could be such a drag, and though they'd only flirted around back in training, he was hopeful for what the evening might bring.

They sat in control, sharing a flask of inexpensive blended synth and catching up. The door to the main observation deck was standing open, the soft night sounds of the jungle floating in on a balmy breeze, and they were alone, except for Evans. Technically, Windy was still on duty until midnight, but there weren't going to be any calls coming in; the most excitement they'd had in months was already parked outside, and Evans was catching a nap in the corner, drooling on his own arm. If Windy got tipped and anything important happened, he'd just wake him up; Evans owed him, anyway.

". . . so I'm screaming emergency, the intake spike is hitching and my VTOL is out, right?" Irwin said. "And the dumb bitch tells me that she can't clear me until I send her my compressor reads."

Windy laughed, keeping his voice low. He didn't want to wake Evans up. "What did you say?"

Irwin grinned. "I told her, 'I'm about to drop six gross of barrel fuel oil all over your goddamn strip,' and if she wanted my reads, she could read them off her own ass after I branded 'em there."

"And what'd she say?"

"She told me I was cleared to land, not even a blink." Irwin sipped from the flask, handing it back to Windy. "I made it down, obviously. But I found out later, she walked the same day. Said she couldn't take the pressure."

Windy laughed again, shaking his head. "She should've taken this job. In the last eight months, I've landed four ships, including that shuttle and you. Most of my working time is spent listening to air and playing cards with Evans, or Tom Cabot . . ."

Irwin raised her arms over her head and stretched as he spoke, a movement that did wonders for his point of view. She caught his appraising look and deliberately shook her chest from side to side, grinning widely.

"Enjoy it, Windy, it's as close as you're going to get," she said sweetly. "Probably."

"Probably?" he asked. "Any chance of upgrading?"

Irwin shrugged, reaching for the whiskey. "We'll see. So, no interesting stories, huh? No wild-animal attacks out here? No secret jungle cults? Station fever?"

Windy sighed. "No. Hey, a couple of our survey guys went missing today, does that count?"

Irwin shook her head. "Probably not . . . although that reminds me, I saw something when I was coming in, couple of klicks that way—" She pointed vaguely south. "Flash of light, real brief."

Windy frowned. "Huh. Maybe that's them. We don't have any perimeter set up, so it had to be—"

Ka-chink!

From just outside, like something metal being dropped onto the deck.

"What's that?" Irwin asked nervously.

Windy didn't know. "Something fell off one of the landing decks, maybe . . ."

There was a shuffling sound, like leaves brushing one of the smaller stabilizing envelopes—and then a soft clattering sound, like a bone rattle being shook underwater. They both stood up, looking toward the open door, Windy suddenly feeling stone sober in spite of how much drink he'd had. Eight months of quiet Bunda nights, learning every natural sound that the planet had to offer, and he'd never heard anything like *that*.

"Something hanging off the platform, scraping the trees or something?" Irwin asked.

Windy shook his head. It was a calm night, and the nav computers automatically adjusted for flux when the wind was blowing. He knew he should take charge, walk out and look around and tell Irwin that it was nothing—but he didn't want to go outside. In fact, he felt quite strongly that it was a shitty idea.

Don't be a wooze, not with her watching!

He was being stupid, and he also knew the longer he waited, the less he'd feel like moving. It was five meters to the door and he could see the deck past it, a piece of railing against a backdrop of darkness. Nothing, there was nothing there.

"Wait here a sec, okay?" He said, finally having shamed himself into heading for the door. Irwin ignored him, following one step behind; he decided that he didn't mind.

Snap out of it, you're too old for this . . .

Windy paused at the door, searching for movement, and saw nothing. He hadn't realized how tense he'd become until he relaxed, the perfectly normal, ordinary sight of nothing at all confirming how paranoid he was. He walked toward the railing, grinning at himself.

"Nothing but me and thee and a shitload of trees,"

he said, and heard Irwin actually giggle behind him. Yeah, tonight was looking good, he couldn't remember having ever heard Kelly Irwin *giggle*—

"Hey, what's this?" he said absently, moving toward the rail. There was a metal claw hanging off of the top bar, like a grappling hook, a taut rope disappearing down into the leafy dark. Was someone actually trying to climb the station? Bullshit. It was possible, the ground was only ten meters down, but who'd want to scale an ME when there was a lift? And even if one of the techs wanted to climb something, the area they'd picked was incredibly dangerous; if they happened to snag one of the stabilizers, they could do some serious damage—

Suddenly, the air in front of his eyes shifted, blurring, and a bitter, oily scent flooded his nostrils, and there was a sound like metal again—

—and then a scream, a howling, feral shriek that was so close Windy could feel its stinking heat across his face, and then heat on his throat, wet and sharp and complete, and then he couldn't stand up anymore.

The sudden scream was terrible, a bestial, animal cry that seemed to come from thin air, and then Windy fell backwards, and all Irwin could see was blood. A pumping, solid sheath of red that was dressing him, enveloping him from the neck down.

"Oh!" It was all she could think, confused and shocked. *He was just standing there and now, now he's—*

There was a distortion in front of her, in the very air; part of the railing seemed closer for just a second, as if it had been magnified, and Irwin heard a trilling sound coming from the distortion, a sound like a choking bird, and she'd seen and heard enough.

She turned, sprinting back into the control room, screaming at the sleeping man in the corner, slamming her hand down on a panel of buttons that might close the door. "Sound the alarm, man down! Man down, something got him, *sound the fuckin' alarm*!"

Behind her, the door dropped shut—and at the same time, the floor shifted violently underfoot, tilting at a fifteen-degree slant before swinging back down. The flask on the console hit the floor, the air filling with the sharp smell of liquor, and from outside, another scream. A clicking, rattling shriek of fury, not human and not alone, another cry rising to join it, and a third.

Irwin spun, desperately searching the thin air for that blurred strangeness, and saw nothing. The sleeper, Evans, was on his feet, stumbling for a control board and asking what had happened, what was happening.

Irwin didn't know, and Windy was surely dead. Shivering, she stumbled to a cabinet in the control room's corner to try and find some kind of a weapon.

The convict was only half-conscious, and Lara had started to insist that there was no download; the psych projections had suggested as much, and also that beating Jess down was the surest path to her eventual submission. Briggs let Keene continue, hoping that she'd give it up before the guard battered him to death; Briggs was a civilized man, and while violence was a valuable and often necessary tool, he didn't particularly enjoy watching it.

Their young teammate only seemed half-conscious himself, staring at the exo suit, lips trembling, as Lara screamed for Keene to stop. It really was fairly brutal. Briggs was starting to think that he'd have to drag the whole lot to the nearest Company lab for an expensive chemical flush when the station suddenly moved. Violently.

Briggs wheeled his arms, grabbing one of the handholds on the wall as the floor settled back down, but at a slight list. Nirasawa still had Lara and Ellis in hand, although Keene had joined Jess on the floor. Vincent was clutching the pilot seat, an expression of alarm replacing the queasy look he'd worn for the last ten minutes.

"Vincent, what's going on?" Briggs demanded, his

heart fluttering from the unexpected jolt. Keene was on his feet again, looking to him for instruction, his knuckles red and swollen.

Vincent shook his head, his eyes wide. "I—I don't know, the whole platform like that, it has to be someone at the main controls."

Wonderful.

"Show me," Briggs said, monumentally irritated by the rude interruption—and a little uncomfortable with the naked fear on Vincent's mousy face.

"Nirasawa, come with me. Keene, stay here. Let our . . . *prisoners* have a moment to think about how they want this to end."

Keene stepped up to take Nirasawa's place, holding Lara and Ellis. It was a setback as far as keeping the pressure on, but Briggs wanted to be here when the woman finally broke. After all the effort he'd put in, he didn't want to miss the moment of triumph.

An alarm was sounding from somewhere lower on the station, an annoying bleat like some small animal being stepped on repeatedly. It bled up into the night sky, making Briggs even more uncomfortable.

What the hell's going on here?

Vincent stepped out onto the platform, Briggs and Nirasawa right behind—and it occurred to him that perhaps he wasn't the only one on Bunda aware of the information on that log. Aware that there were billions to be made for anyone— any corporation—with access to hard stats on infestation.

No, he'd been careful, the Company had it all locked down—

—but there are enemies within.

Someone like Julia Russ, maybe. Or any one of a dozen competitors he could think of, desperate for that spot on the Board. Weyland/Yutani wanted results, they didn't necessarily care who handed them in.

Briggs turned, leaning back into the stale shuttle air. "Watch for strangers," he said.

Keene, towering over his two charges, Jess at his feet, nodded briskly. It would have to do.

Briggs turned back to Vincent, motioning impatiently for him to lead the way—and deciding, quite firmly, that it was the monotonous scream of the station's alarm that was making him feel so anxious.

When the ME shook, Tom Cabot was hiding out in the rec room, watching a sci-fi holovid in near dark with a few of the researchers—Cindy and Di, both paleo women, and John C., one of the maintenance guys. The sudden up and down wasn't too bad where they were, all of them managed to keep their seats, but Cabot knew that parts of the station would have been harder hit.

The second it stopped, all of them were on their feet, moving toward the open door that led out onto the rec platform. The floor was slanted just a bit, Cabot could feel it, and when he heard the stabilizer alarm start up, he felt real fear. MEs weren't supposed to quake like that, and something had to be seriously wrong if the nav computers couldn't keep the alarm from sounding.

Either someone entered a drift code or we got caught on something big, something heavy, and it just had *to happen with a suit on board, didn't it? First time ever and Vincent'll be having a shit fit . . .*

They reached the door, moving out onto the platform littered with bolted tables and chairs, Cabot stepping up to the railing. John C. and the two scientists joined him, identical expressions of nervous concern on their faces. The rec deck overlooked control directly, maybe they'd be able to see something—

"What's that?" Cindy said, pointing to the deck below. The outside lights were low, it was hard to tell, a sprawl of something wet, shining darkly . . .

"Oh, *shit*," Di said weakly. "It's Windy, that's Windy."

They stared down at what was left of the channel

watcher, no chance that he was alive with all of that *blood*—

—and behind them, something shrieked. A gurgling, unbridled howl, a scream of murder about to happen.

Cabot spun and saw nothing at all, but the horrible sound went on, erupting out of thin air, and then they were all stumbling away from the rail, running for the tunnel that opened out onto the deck, that would take them away from the invisible screamer—

—and Cindy, closest to the corridor, let out a strangled cry and stopped cold, her head whipping back as if she'd run into something, her limbs flailing wildly. All of them pulled to a stop only a couple of meters behind her, clutching at each other like frightened children.

"What is it, what's happening?" John C. screamed, and no one answered, watching in shocked terror as metal claws appeared in front of Cindy, from *nowhere*, a sharp sliding sound, and then they were swooping down from above, raking her open from throat to belly. Blood gushed out and hit the platform with a wet *slap*, and Cindy collapsed, crashing facefirst into the sudden lake of red.

Cabot didn't waste time wondering. He grabbed at John C. and Di, giving them a jerk before spinning around and sprinting for the door back into the rec room. He didn't turn back to see if they were following, didn't care, all he wanted was to get the fuck away from whatever had clawed Cindy open, *oh, please God, Buddha, Jesus don't let me die*—

Behind him, an alien howl, a caterwaul of triumph, and he was going to make it, the door was *right there*—

—and the crazy hope that crashed through him as he burst into the dimly lit room was the last thing he felt, except for the unseen arm that clamped down across his throat, except for the slick, hot sensation of being drained as something cold slipped through his abdomen.

18

Noguchi was dozing, a light, restless sleep that seemed to be taking her in and out of unpleasant dreams, when the aging wave scanner started spitting out static and words.

Startled out of her doze, Noguchi rolled over to switch it off, wondering why she'd bothered to put the damned thing on in the first place. She touched the controls, then paused, her attention caught by the sound of the speaker's voice. A woman, and she sounded scared.

". . . Bunda survey, we are . . . tack . . . lizers malfunctioning . . ."

It was clearer than Noguchi was used to, the words sharper. She hit the tuner rather than the power switch and upped the volume a notch, then lay back down on her bunk, listening. With the channel reestablished, the connection cleared up a little.

". . . peat, this is Bunda survey . . . are under attack, send help! The station . . . ucked up, I can . . . people screaming . . . ey're invisible, can't see them and . . ."

Noguchi sat up, staring at the scanner.

". . . killing everyone . . ."

Invisible. Attack.

Hunters.

Even through her shocked disbelief, it only took a second for everything to fall into place. The truth was so simple.

Wouldn't want me along on a Hunt where the grand finale involves killing humans, would you?

". . . can hear me, I'm gonna try to see . . . can get to . . . ships, evacuate . . ."

She barely heard it, the thoughts too sudden and overwhelming, blocking out everything else. The warrior with the wrist banner, Topknot's decision for her to fight a novice on the morning of the Hunt, the consistent and all-consuming hatred that they'd held for her, from the beginning. What Hunter befriends their prey? Sharpening their skills on bugs, ranting on and on about the Hunter's code and the Blooding ritual, and maybe some of that was true—but the big Hunt, the one that brought Leaders and their veteran comrades in from throughout their universe . . .

. . . *humans. They went down there to slaughter people.*

For a moment, Noguchi couldn't move, her body stiff with the desperate need to do *something*, every muscle locked because she didn't know what that thing was. The transports were all gone, there was no way for her to get to the surface—but she couldn't do nothing, listening to some terrified woman screaming for help while she sat and waited for the Hunters to return . . .

Topknot, her Leader. She'd *respected* him, and the pain of that thought turned to an anger deeper than mere emotion; her very soul had been betrayed, she'd suffered a year of hell adhering to a code created by hypocrites. By human killers.

Noguchi stood up and walked to the shelf in the corner of the little room before she knew what she was going to do, pulling down things that had been given to her by the Hunters. There was the blade with the shortened handle, the knee and shoulder pads that had been a child yautja's, a dull erose knife that she'd spent hours sharpening and polishing, honing to a sparkling sharpness. Throwaways from the Clan that she'd been proud to own . . .

She didn't have a plan as she started to dress, slipping into her armor, feeling stronger with each layer of splash suit and weaponry, the aches and pains of her body falling away. By the time she was finished, enough of an idea had formed that she was ready to act.

Noguchi was going to make her break with the Hunters in a way that they would never forget, and she was going to make peace with herself while she was doing it. When it was over, she would truly be free.

At last, Briggs and the others were gone and there was only Keene, watching them, holding Ellis's numb shoulder with a grip like a steel vise. Lara's, too, her lovely face lined with pain.

Ellis felt dizzy and sick and ashamed. Jess had been badly hurt and now Briggs didn't believe that there was no ship's log. Through all of it, the only thing that seemed clear—figuratively and literally—was Max. Max stood giant and invulnerable, watching it all, its hydraulic body almost glowing with energy at rest. Max had been the answer, and Ellis had ignored it.

I was afraid of pain, of dying, and I failed to act. If we were together, none of this would have happened, we could have stopped this before anyone was hurt. He'd been weak, he'd already forgotten what Max had taught him . . .

On the floor, Jess moaned. Ellis looked away from Max, feeling a physical ache in his stomach at the sight of his friend. Jess was on his back, his swollen eyes closed.

"Jess? Are you—can you hear me?" Lara asked, and let out a small cry as Keene gave her a rough shake. Jess cracked his eyes open, rolling slowly onto his side, breathing shallowly.

"Yeah," he said, wincing. "Yeah, I hear you . . ."

"Stay on the floor," Keene ordered, his Nordic face still flushed from beating Jess, from exertion or pleasure or both. "Get up and I'll kill you."

Ellis looked at Max again, feeling as though his heart would break. They'd been getting closer since their joining, their thoughts running through his mind now and he'd been a fool, Max still had multiple—

—11.52, one hundred M309 rounds each—

—cartridges for the pulse rifle, at least twenty HEAP grenades left, and most of its secondary M210 tank was still full of napthal. Worst of all, Ellis knew that feeling sorry for what he hadn't done didn't matter at all, it didn't help and they were still going to be killed by Briggs for information that they didn't even have—

"Ellis, what's wrong?" Lara said sharply, a thread of terror in her voice.

Ellis turned his head, confused, saw that both Keene and Lara were looking at him—

—and then Lara was moving, bending her knees and slipping out from beneath Keene's hand, coming up from her crouch with her arm straight, her hand flat—

—and Ellis felt Keene's fingers clench and relax on his shoulder as Lara chopped the side of her hand into his throat, a sound like some crisp vegetable being snapped erupting from the blond's quivering lips. He grabbed at his neck with both hands, his eyes wide, his face purpling in seconds.

Lara was in a fighting stance, her hands up, ready to hit again—but Keene was no longer a threat. He crumpled to the floor still clutching at his throat, his mouth opening and closing soundlessly. A few seconds later, he wasn't moving at all.

Ellis crouched next to him, putting a shaky hand over Keene's mouth. He wasn't breathing.

"You killed him," Ellis said wonderingly.

Lara was already moving toward Jess, rubbing at her shoulder. "I used to be a Marine," she said. "People seem to keep forgetting that."

Together, they knelt next to Jess, Lara helping him to sit up. Jess groaned again but managed to stay upright, holding his head in his hands. He squinted at Lara from red eyes, the welts on his face already darkening to black.

"Jesus. Remind me not to fuck with you," he said softly.

Lara smiled a little. "Yeah, well. I was tired of waiting for you to make your move."

The floor of the shuttle trembled, the platform beneath seeming to tilt a little more. The distant alarm continued to blare. Jess finally raised his head and sat up straight, gritting his teeth against his pain.

"We gotta get out of here," he said. "Can we take off?"

Lara shook her head. "We wouldn't make it more than a few klicks, we need to refuel. And we don't have VTOL, I have to program some kind of a flight plan."

Jess looked at Ellis, studying his face. "Kid, you with us?"

Ellis nodded, not sure what Jess was asking, knowing only that he had to make up for his failure. "Yeah. Of course."

With help from both of them, Jess crawled to his feet, swaying for a moment—

—.37—

—before he found his balance. Lara crouched next to Keene and rifled through his suit, pulling out the semiautomatic that had been taken earlier.

"Get on the program," Jess said. "Ellis, I'm going to need your help. Come on."

Ellis nodded, wondering why so much of this felt like a dream, why the numbers in his mind wouldn't stay, wouldn't take the place of the turbulent and unpleasant emotions that continued to plague him. He felt confused and unsure of himself—but as he followed Jess out into the strange night, he swore that he wouldn't give in to his feelings, and that whatever it took, he wouldn't screw up again.

Johnathon Callistori, aka John C., made it to control without going outside again, using one of the maintenance stairwells and coming in from the corridor that led to the central lift. The door had been blocked, but he was let in once he'd screamed his name a few times, babbling his story out to the scared young archaeologist who opened the door. He'd had to jump over Cabot's body, dragging Di along with him, and before they made it to the tunnel she had been grabbed away, hot blood from her cut throat splashing against the backs of his legs as he crawled into the dark.

Control was packed, people crying and semihysterical and pale with shock. Windy and then two others had been murdered just outside, the sight of their bloody bodies feeding their collective terror. Cabot was dead, Vincent wasn't there, and there were a few more screaming, pounding knocks at the inner door, frightened researchers tumbling in with stories of alien howls and invisible beings, of friends and coworkers slain. In all, it took a few moments for any kind of order to be established. One of the pilots, Lee Goldmann, finally called for a head count. There were thirteen Bunda people missing, eight confirmed dead, and no one had any idea what had attacked them.

Goldmann and the other Bunda pilot, Les Drucker, called for an immediate evac. No one disagreed, except for Chris Aquino, who didn't want to leave without his missing lover, and a woman named Irwin, the Sun Jumper pilot who was waiting for her boss to show up. John C. thought they were nuts, but then, he wasn't all that sure of his own sanity anymore; the feel of Di's blood cooling against his calves was a nightmare like no other, turning part of his mind into a vague and shadowy place that he did his best to stay out of.

Goldmann took charge, sending two of the more together biotechs to the supply room for what weapons Bunda had and getting Evans to set up the AD signal on a pulse to the next outpost. Once they were armed, they'd move out to the transports en masse and go. There was no real discussion about waiting for the missing few to show, the subject unanimously ignored; maybe they'd hear the ships warming up and make it out to the LZ in time to board. If they didn't, they were probably dead already.

Together, they waited for Karen and Rich to get back with weapons, silent and afraid as they listened to the open intercom, listened for screams. After Evans had sent out their auto-distress, he tried to get some of the others to join him in prayer, but he didn't have many takers. John C., a lapsed Catholic, thought that if Evans had seen what *he* had, he'd realize that God had nothing to do with what had happened on Bunda; the Devil was more like it, the planet his now. If God had any interest at all in taking care of matters, there was going to be a war—and all John C. wanted was to get the hell out of Their way.

19

Noguchi walked purposefully through the ship, the three yautja she passed ignoring her completely. If they saw the burner strapped to her back, they didn't think it important. She'd been dishonored, after all; what did they care if she chose to wander around in full armor, armed or not? That was her assumption, anyway, and all that mattered was that no one try to stop her as she made her way to operations.

The *Shell*'s control room wasn't overly large, one long console running the length of the room with two bolted chairs, a wide front viewscreen, and the main terminal for the ship's computer. Everything in Clan culture was based around the Hunt, their technology advanced enough to make things like piloting extremely simple; Hunters didn't waste time or energy in areas where there was no honor to be gained.

She stood just outside control in the large, empty shuttle dock where Topknot's transport usually sat, preparing herself for her first action. The two yautja in operations were older Hunters, past their prime, as most shipworkers seemed to be. The attitude of yautja toward their elders was respectful, a kind of unspoken understanding existing that the "retired" *could* Hunt, but had simply decided not to; in this way, old Hunters that weren't lucky enough to have died in battle were still worthy of regard.

They don't Hunt anymore, but that doesn't mean they're any less dangerous. If anything, the fact that they'd survived to become old in such a violent culture spoke very highly of their skills. They wouldn't be expecting to be attacked on a ship, but she'd still have to be fast and efficient, not a movement wasted.

The door was open, making it easier for her to slip silently into the room, walking on the balls of her padded feet. Neither of the Hunters turned away from the console or from their conversation, probably trading stories of trophy Hunts. They were dressed only in harness tops and loincloths, no weapons within reach, and Noguchi managed to get within a meter before one of them noticed her. It was one of the few Hunters whose name she could actually pronounce, Prient'de, and he broke off talking, his tusks flaring wide with alarm—

—and Noguchi snapped out her wrist blades even as she swung, catching Prient'de under his chin in a swift and sure killing strike, dropping to one knee and turning, hand coming up as droplets of pale blood flew—

—and she rammed the wet blades into the other's lower belly as he rose, realizing too late that the ooman had come to kill them. She'd never named this other, and as he clutched at the strange coils of gut that slid between his claws, toppling, hissing weakly, she thought that "Dead" suited him quite well. The light green, thin liquid that served as yautja blood was hot and smelled almost sweet, the scent filling the room as it flowed across the floor.

No going back, she was committed, and the thought made her own blood run hot. She didn't feel proud of having killed the unarmed Hunters, but there was no guilt, either. She felt driven, she felt alive with intent, and there was a sense of righteousness in her heart that she knew would only get stronger.

Noguchi walked back to the door and closed it, pushing the lock control and turning the manual bolt. Given time and tools, the Hunters could get through— but she had a diversion in mind, something to take their minds off of the fact that they'd been hijacked.

No time like the present. She sat in front of the console, lifting the arm control from next to one of the small, circular monitors. The system activated; a series of symbols scrolled across the screen on a backdrop of red. Topknot had shown her once how their system worked, and he was going to regret it.

If I can figure out what does what . . .

The *Shell*'s system—and probably all yautja drives, she didn't know—was image-based, each tiny picture a representation of an action or thing. All she had to do was access the right area and connect the symbols in the correct order.

She touched the sensor "pen" to a silhouette of a yautja ship and another set of images popped up—a claw, a mask, lines representing doors, other symbols that she didn't know. There was an egg in the set, and she tapped that one; this time, the image of the queen came up, surrounded by new pictures.

She touched the queen, connecting it to a hand, what looked like a series of knots, a triangle, and back to the queen. There was a flash of green light, a warning with new options available; Noguchi repeated the series and this time there was no warning flash. Instead, the image of the queen appeared alone—and from the symbols that scrolled out beneath, she saw that she had been successful.

Bam bam bam!

Startled, Noguchi turned, saw a pair of faces through the thick window in the door, their mouths moving and mandibles flexing. They'd discovered her sooner than she'd expected, but it didn't matter—or it wouldn't, in a few moments. One of them signaled "stop," fist out in front, and Noguchi turned away. Turned back to the screen, hoping that piloting the ship would be as easy as releasing the queen.

So now she knew what it felt like to be an outcast from two worlds. She'd turned her back on humanity because she'd never felt at home there, and now, by her own hand, she'd erased what Broken Tusk's mark meant to the Clan. She would be Hunted by them, actively, and if they caught her, she wouldn't die quickly.

In that moment, she decided that she was happier than she'd ever been in her life.

If he hadn't had the shit so thoroughly kicked out of him, Jess probably could have managed to refuel the *Nemesis* shuttle on his own; not as fast as with two experienced people, but having to walk Ellis through the process took a few minutes. Each passing second stretched like eternity, and though Jess's anger had only increased with the beating, he felt like he'd learned his lesson on letting it get the better of him, at least for the moment. They had to get gone. Briggs and his other guard could be back at any time, with reinforcements.

And if that's not incentive enough, something is very fucking wrong with this picture.

The tilted platform, the strange rustlings in the trees far below, the alarm that wouldn't shut off. It wasn't possible, but the station had a deserted feel to it, as if everyone had mysteriously disappeared. On the plus side, the freaky circumstances had stirred enough adrenaline through his bruised body that he was capable of moving. But there was also a feeling in the air like death, like no matter what they did, their future didn't include making it off Bunda.

And it won't, if we don't get some fuel loaded into this thing . . .

Everything was ready on his end, flow rate adjusted, the mixture and filtering set. Jess looked away from the control console, over to where Ellis was trying to fit the hose into the shuttle's tank opening. Jess watched for a second and was about to call out for the kid to twist the damn connector to the right when Ellis got it. The line hooked, Jess hit the pump switch.

Lara leaned out of the shuttle, looking as nervous as Jess felt. "What's the holdup? Prelaunch is done, we're a go." She kept her voice low, her gaze darting left and right.

Jess started to give her a thumbs-up, wincing instead as his shoulder recommended otherwise. Every part of him hurt. "We're on, three minutes," he said.

Lara went back in, Jess turning his attention back to the fuel gauges on the console. Three minutes, and they'd be on their way. Even with the air filters cleaned and a full tank, they'd be facing death again within a week—but not at the hands of the Company, and that felt like the best they could hope for—

"*Jess, look out!*" Ellis screamed.

Jess looked up, confused, the kid was staring in his direction but there was nothing around. *Ellis finally snapped—*

Wham!

Something hit Jess's shoulder, hard, knocking him to the deck, the new pain brilliant and sharp. Jess clutched at his arm and looked up, saw nothing—

—except the air, moving. As if it had taken a tangible form, a shifting, living, creature, and he could just make out what looked like twisted knots of hair but much too high, no man was that tall—

"*Get away!*"

The kid, screaming, and the strange, bitter smell hovering around the invisible monster was suddenly overwhelmed by the dizzying fumes of ship fuel. Jess heard liquid hitting the ground, heard Lara calling from inside the shuttle as the air creature moved, turning toward Ellis—

—and Ellis was suddenly only a few meters away, his young face contorted by fear and purpose, the dripping, arm-thick hose in his hands. Before Jess could do any more than sit up, Ellis opened the nozzle all the way, a blast of oily fuel shooting out at the shifting thing.

At once, Jess saw the creature outlined in the powerful river of liquid—a giant after all, humanoid, staggered by the fluid jet pounding at its massive chest. Ellis was struggling to keep hold of the whipping hose, the creature struggling to escape the blast—

—and Jess heard the sharp electric *crack* come from the creature, from its invisible cloak, and saw the shuddering change as parts of it became clear. Jess covered his face, screaming for Ellis to shut it off, to get back, and—

BA-BOOM!

—the bright, white orange night turned to thoughtless black and Jess followed it down, the monster's dying howl chasing him into unconsciousness.

They'd moved out in groups of four and five, each group equipped with at least one weapon, each pale, terrified individual trying to watch all directions at once. All they had were shotguns, practically antiques, but Irwin didn't mind so much; beat the shit out of nothing at all, and one of the groups had agreed to come with her, to wait on board the Sun Jumper for Briggs. The rest of the researchers, scientists, and both Bunda pilots had headed off for the orbiter transports, docked near the top of the station.

Two men and a woman had come with Irwin, one of the men almost catatonic with fear; she and the other man, John something, had to drag him most of the way to the Jumper while the woman guarded. Beneath the droning alarm the night was strangely silent, as if all the life on Bunda was holding its breath, hiding from whatever demons had come. The woman, a redhead named Tia, carried the shotgun with the grim, nononsense expression of a veteran soldier. Irwin was glad to have her along.

Once they were in, the hatch closed, Irwin warmed up the ship and joined the other three in the cabin, the viewscreen dialed to show the platform outside. The fear-struck scientist was already strapped in, his eyes blank and empty, but Tia and John seemed okay. No one approached, the faraway sounds of the transports taking off the only change in the strange air. They watched for what seemed like hours, although it couldn't have been more than a few minutes—and when the platform shook beneath them, a glow of orange light rising up past one of the envelopes along with the dull, muffled sound of an explosion, her companions had had enough waiting.

"If that was a stabilizer, the slant's about to get a fuckload worse," John said, turning to Irwin. "And if one of the envelopes gets blown through, the whole station's going down."

"Maybe your guy was on one of the transports," Tia said hopefully.

Irwin nodded slowly. Maybe he was. And if he wasn't, maybe it was because he was dead, and she wasn't so hot on the idea of joining him.

"Strap in," she said, and the relief on both their faces lent conviction to her decision. She was the pilot, these people were counting on her to take them to safety; Briggs and his twin goons were on their own.

Irwin snapped off the viewscreen and moved toward the cockpit, harnessing in and taking a final check on her passengers before she realized that she hadn't had time to think about what had happened to Windy. It had all happened so fast.

And we were going to be together, we both wanted it, and now it will never happen. He'll never laugh at another one of my dumb stories, or drink to old times or kiss a woman, ever again—he's over, like some movie, dead.

Irwin brought the Jumper up, a tear running down her face for the terrible murder of her friend as they blasted away from Bunda survey.

•   •   •

Vincent was nearly hysterical when they finally made it to control, and Briggs had to suppress a serious urge to scream at him. It was bad enough that the ASM had led them halfway around the station trying to find a lift that worked, babbling all the way about what a Company man he was. But at the sight of the corpses on the outside platform, followed by the sounds of Bunda's transport ships taking off, he'd graduated from annoying to a possible liability.

They stood in control, Vincent pacing and tearful, his voice raised to a near shout.

"I don't understand, who could have done this? Why, why would anyone want to kill them, why didn't someone call us, why did they leave? Jesus, I don't understand, where's Cabot, he wouldn't have left without trying to find us and—"

"Shut *up*," Briggs snapped, almost as irritated with himself as with the blithering Vincent. He hadn't expected such a savage attack, hadn't been prepared for it, and God only knew what was happening to the three on the shuttle.

"Nirasawa, this station is under attack by person or persons unknown," he said briskly. "Get me back to the *Nemesis* shuttle by the fastest possible route."

"Yes, Mr. Briggs," Nirasawa said, turning back to the outside platform. Briggs followed him, stepping over one of the extraordinarily dead people and wrinkling his nose in disgust. All three had been eviscerated, which didn't strike him as the work of a Company exec—leading him to the unsettling conclusion that some outside competition was involved.

Vincent tagged after them, finally quiet, and as they reached the steps leading up to the next deck—

BA-BOOM!

Nirasawa reached back and gripped Briggs's arm before he could fall as the platform trembled violently, continuing its gradual slant. Briggs could see a reflected glow off the side of one of the spheres. Something was on fire, something in the direction of the H/K shuttle.

They'd have to hurry, these stations wouldn't withstand a serious fire and with no one to put it out, it was only a matter of time—

"The whole platform's going to crash," Vincent said.

Brilliant.

"I don't understand," the ASM whined, stumbling up the stairs behind them. "Why would anyone—"

Briggs cut him off, tired of waiting for Vincent to figure out what was right in front of him. "Think about it—your survey hasn't turned up anything of particular value, has it . . . yet someone has deemed it necessary to attack your station and kill your people, on the very same day that a shuttle from the *Nemesis* lands. Tell me—do you really think Weyland/Yutani is the only corporation interested in the data they collected?"

They reached the top of the steps and started across another deck, the flickering glow getting stronger. Across the wide, empty expanse of dark platform was another set of stairs. Briggs sighed, feeling entirely put out with the circumstances, with the idiot botanist and the obstinate Lara and with whatever internal leak had led to the immensely inconvenient attack on Bunda's station.

"You mean another *company* did this?" Vincent asked, his attempt at outrage coming out in a squeak.

Nirasawa had stopped, his head cocked as if listening for something. Briggs glanced back at Vincent, wondering what he could possibly say that would make him be quiet. Nothing, he imagined, some people were just—

"Sir—trouble," Nirasawa said, and stepped forward with his arms raised, reaching out as if to grab a shadow. Briggs frowned, peering into the darkness—

—and suddenly, out of nowhere, a giant appeared. He was dressed in some kind of armor with long, beaded hair surrounding a full face mask. He towered over Nirasawa by half a meter, and the guard was by no means a small man.

A cloaking device!

"Wh—what is it?" Vincent stammered.

"Synthetic," Briggs said, unable to keep the awe out of his voice as Nirasawa grabbed the giant's arms, straining to hold him in place. Nirasawa was state, his vat-grown muscles fibered with steel thread, the combination of electrical stim and pumped microhydraulics providing him with exceptional power; Briggs had wanted two of them, but there simply weren't enough of his model to meet the demand. That the assailant seemed to be holding his own was simply amazing, and with an *invisibility* device . . . this was big, he'd have to get a team on it as soon as possible.

"I'll hold him, Mr. Briggs," Nirasawa said, barely able to restrain the monster synth. "I would recommend you get to your Sun Jumper—"

The attacker slipped one hand free and slashed at Nirasawa's face, divots of layered flesh flying. The guard managed to restrain him again, but Briggs realized that he was right; the 949 log wouldn't do him any good if he were killed in a station explosion or murdered by one of these cloaked soldiers.

Back to the ship, wait for Nirasawa, and then have him fetch Keene and the others, we can conclude our business on the way back to Earth . . .

"Vincent, take point, I don't know the layout," Briggs said, reluctant to tear his gaze from the struggle. Truly astounding. There was a clattering sound coming from the strangely dressed synth, perhaps some malfunction. If Nirasawa could incapacitate it, carry it back to—

"But—Mr. Briggs, isn't that your ship?"

That got his attention. Briggs's head whipped around, his gaze following Vincent's pointing finger. For a second, he couldn't believe what he was seeing, unable to comprehend that Irwin would *dare*—but the elite Jumper was speeding away from the station, its sleek form unmistakable against the starry sky.

Damn her, when I get back to Earth, I'll—

When he got back. Of course he *would*, but suddenly, he wasn't so sure that he should be worrying about what he would do to Irwin at some future date. There were more immediate concerns—and for the first time since he'd landed on this forsaken hole, for the first time in *years*, he had no idea what the next step should be.

20

The force of the explosion pushed Jess underneath the shuttle, lucky for him; as it was, Lara had to slap out a patch of burning fabric on his leg before dragging him away from the growing fire.

She wasn't sure what had happened, she'd heard Ellis shout and then there was the explosion, the shuttle rocking violently. She'd run out and seen Ellis frantically pulling the hose away from the ship, huge sections of the deck covered with burning fuel. She'd seen a flailing shape engulfed in flames only a few meters away, and for one terrible second, she'd been sure that it was Jess. If she hadn't heard him groaning from beneath the transport . . .

Ellis joined them behind the shuttle, helping Lara pull Jess to the far railing, but Lara knew that they wouldn't be safe if the tanks caught fire. Jess started to come out of his daze, looking up into Ellis's stricken face as he rubbed at his jaw, obviously in pain.

"Ever heard of overkill, kid?" he asked.

Lara laughed weakly. Jess was okay, that was the important thing—but the realization that they weren't going to be flying anywhere was sinking in, making her feel very, very tired.

God, is this ever going to end?

"What happened?" Lara asked.

"I think I killed us," Ellis said, so softly that Lara barely heard it. "There was this—thing, it attacked Jess . . ."

He trailed off miserably, the dancing light of the developing fire on his face making him look incredibly old. Lara put the rest together quickly enough; he'd sprayed the assailant with fuel and somehow, something had caught fire.

"It was invisible," Jess said, using the rail to drag himself to his feet. "Some kind of electrical device, got shorted out and *boom*."

Lara couldn't find it in herself to be surprised. A personal cloaking mechanism? Sure, why not, it was no stranger than corporate mass murder, no more improbable than being fished out of the abyss on a dead shuttle in the first place.

There was a soft humming overhead and they all looked up to see a small ship go streaking across the dark, close enough for them to see the Weyland/Yutani logo. Lara thought she'd heard other ships earlier . . .

. . . *and what are the chances that there's still anyone left willing to give us a lift? Or anyone at all?* If there were people around, they sure weren't interested in putting out the fire that was currently consuming one of their landing decks.

"Briggs?" Jess asked, still watching as the ship shot away from the station.

Lara nodded. "Probably." She didn't say what she was thinking, what Jess and Ellis surely already knew. If a high suit like Briggs, who'd wanted them so much that he'd come to Bunda himself was giving it up—

—then things here are bad, really fuckin' bad.

Maybe the thing that had attacked Jess had been busy with the researchers, before; that might explain the ceaseless alarm, anyway. Or maybe it was just the fact that the station's platforms had continued their slow tilt, at least fifteen degrees now; if they slanted much farther, there wouldn't be a stable deck to take off from.

"We gotta get out of here before the shuttle catches," Jess said, although he didn't look well enough to do much more than stand upright. And Ellis looked like he was on the verge of some emotional collapse, his entire body trembling, his eyes wide and shining with unshed tears.

"I'm so sorry," he said, taking a step away from them, his hands clenched into fists. "This is all my fault."

"Hey, I might've done the same thing," Lara said, "or Jess. It's—"

"You don't *understand*," he said, his voice rising, "I've done everything wrong since we got here, *everything*!"

Instinctively, Lara took a step toward him, reaching out—

—and there was a sound so deep, so powerful, that they felt it as much as heard it, *WHOOOF*, an explosion of brilliant light, a massive wave of pressure that threw all of them against the waist-high railing. The deck beneath them slanted past forty-five degrees, all of them falling, landing and skidding—

"Hang on!" Jess shouted, but there was nothing to hang on *to*. The deck was lit up like day and Lara rolled over, trying desperately to find a handhold on the slick platform. She saw the shuttle, burning, crashing across the deck and blowing right through the railing, a giant, tearing metal sound as it plunged over the side. She saw Ellis and Jess, scrabbling to hang on, saw both of them slide beneath the high rail, disappearing after the shuttle—

—and she saw the burning envelope, an incredible fireball of ignited gas, the flame eating the pliable shell like acid through paper. It was the last thing she saw as she slipped over the side, falling through the shadow of the crashing station.

Within moments of her release, the alien queen had exacted her revenge on at least a handful of her captors; nine, to be exact, the only Hunters left on board. Noguchi was too busy flying the *Shell* to watch all of it, but she saw enough. The queen had somehow known where the yautja were gathered, and made her way unerringly to the dock outside of the pilot's room. How she'd negotiated the lifts and tunnels, Noguchi didn't know or care.

The ship hadn't yet broken through Bunda's atmosphere when Noguchi heard the queen's shriek, a furious and somehow gleeful cry, echoing through the hollow dock. It pierced the clattering shouts of the yautja trying to break into the control room, the sounds of metal banging against the door cutting off in a heartbeat. She heard the Hunters cry warnings to one another, heard and felt the queen's thundering approach, and felt a kind of perverse satisfaction at the thought of what would happen next.

They won't use burners, not on a queen. Not without Topknot's leave. And all of them, experienced veterans . . . Noguchi couldn't deny the curiosity she felt, wondering how they'd fare against the loosed queen. She finished with her "programming," directing the *Shell* to home in on the signal from Topknot's craft, and hurried to the hatch's window. The battle was already in progress, three Hunters down, dying or dead. Six were left, and they'd circled the raging queen with makeshift weapons, mallets, pry bars, a kind of pickax with one sharpened end; two of them were holding lengths of braided rope, and none wore armor of any kind.

Stupid and arrogant. Any sympathy Noguchi might have felt for them was pretty much wiped out by the simple fact that they were still there; instead of leaving, locking the queen inside and waiting for reinforcements to return—or just killing her outright, for that matter—they meant to capture her again, without even bothering to arm themselves properly.

The queen, crouched in their midst, was swinging her head slowly back and forth, tilting it as if to mark their positions. Her tail curled restlessly about her giant, clawed feet, its razor tip leaving long scratches in the deck's floor, occasionally slapping against one of the dead yautja nearby. He'd been clawed open, his chest a muddled soup of bone and green, and the queen's tail whipped streamers of his blood across the legs of some of those circling her.

Noguchi saw one of the Hunters behind the watchful bug, Beads, signal to another, one of the rope holders; he was going to attack, and wanted both of the rope holders to move in while the queen was distracted. Noguchi watched as the signal went around the circle, each of the Hunters picking it up—

—and as if she understood that *they* were distracted by their own foolish planning, the queen lunged forward, her tail coiling up behind her. She snatched at the nearest Hunter with both sets of ebony claws on her right side, her talons sliding into his chest before he could raise his pry bar. At the same time, her tail slashed out, knocking Beads and two others to the deck. The sharp tip cut through tendon and bone, crippling Beads and the Hunter to his left. One of Beads's feet was completely sliced off, toppling over into the gush of pale liquid that spurted from his ankle.

In a single move, she'd halved the group. With a feral scream, she flung the limp Hunter hanging from her right hands away, his body smashing into one wall hard enough for Noguchi to hear the bones snapping, even through the door.

A Hunter she'd called Inu seized the opportunity, leaping forward with his "pick," burying the sharp end in the top of the screeching queen's left thigh. Even as a trickle of her blood started its bubbling erosion of the metal, Inu was lifted off his feet and held up in front of her grinning, drooling face. Her inner jaws shot out, tearing into Inu's forehead, snapping closed and with-drawing in the blink of an eye. The Hunter's limbs were still spasming when she threw him aside—

—and the *Shell* pitched forward suddenly, knock-ing the two yautja still standing to the floor, causing the queen to stumble. Noguchi grabbed at the door's handle, managing to keep upright. She turned, saw that the *Shell* was tunneling through Bunda's outer at-mosphere, flashes of light and dark painting the view-screen with violent, burning motion.

Another trumpeting howl from the queen. Nogu-chi turned back to the window just in time to see the bug mother put an end to the ill-planned assault—a step forward, a swift blow delivered, a lash of her tail, and it was over. The deck was awash with green, bro-ken bodies toppled together, unmoving. If the two crip-pled Hunters were still alive, Noguchi couldn't tell. And the queen—

Noguchi took a step back from the door as her long, midnight face filled the window, as she seemed to look into the control room. To look directly at *her*, her black comb sweeping up and out of sight, her grinning blind-ness tilted to smell or taste or hear the woman inside.

Noguchi studied her, filled with awe, afraid to breathe. She was a glorious, terrible creature, she was Death, the Black Warrior that the Hunters spoke of be-fore battle.

For a frozen moment, they faced each other, a handwidth of clear plastic separating them—and then the monstrous queen turned and moved away, a dark grace in her fluid, powerful movements. Noguchi watched her disappear from the bloody dock, feeling as though she'd been spared, not knowing why.

Behind her, the console gurgled out a few yautja words, telling her that manual assistance was required to set exact coordinates. Noguchi turned and moved back to the controls, surprised to see the night sky of Bunda flashing by on the large viewscreen. It had taken less time than she'd thought . . .

Still dazed from her closeness to the alien queen, it took her a moment to see the bright spot on the monitor, a yellow-white flower in the dark jumble of the planet's surface, as big or bigger than the *Shell*.

What—

An explosion, and a big one. Noguchi checked the monitor for Topknot's ship signal, and although she couldn't be sure she was reading it right, it appeared that he wasn't more than a few klicks from the fireball. In any case, it was obvious where the action on Bunda was centered.

Noguchi tapped at the controls, shifting the ship toward the light, hoping that she wasn't too late.

Kevin Vincent woke up hurting and alone, the bright heat from the burning station illuminating the crash of bushes he'd landed in. He tried to move, to sit up, but felt a sharp, stabbing pain across his back, centering on his left shoulder. He was able to turn his head, at least, enough to see the mass of flaming wreckage that had been Bunda survey. It seemed to stretch forever, klicks of smashed deck, klicks of burning, stinking envelope draped across mountains of debris.

"Shit," he whispered miserably, feeling terrible in every way possible. His station had been attacked, his people murdered for information about some abominable experiment, and those who'd survived had fled, leaving him to die. Briggs was probably dead, no real comfort since he'd be held responsible, he seemed to have broken his shoulder—

—and I'm lying in a goddamn bush and it's poking through my goddamn shirt and it HURTS, and why doesn't someone just put me out of my goddamn misery?

If he didn't move, the pain wasn't too bad. Vincent closed his eyes for a moment, sweat rolling off of his flushed skin, wondering what could possibly happen next. That he'd survived was a small miracle—not because of the fall; the station had gone down slowly enough for the fall to be survivable—but that the gods hadn't killed him already, just on general principles.

Because that would've been too easy, gotta let me live so I can understand how much they hate me, let me suffer a little more. No fun if I don't suffer . . .

The crackle and hiss of the giant, shallow fire was loud enough to occupy his hearing until the *crack* of a thin branch not two meters away reached him. He instinctively tried to sit up, and was instantly knocked back by the pain.

"Owww, no, no, no, don't wanna die, please—" Vincent babbled out a stream of denial and wishes, eyes squenched shut, knowing that whatever was coming wasn't coming to help.

He was right. The thing that stood over him when he opened his eyes was the thing from the station, the synth that had been fighting Briggs's bodyguard—except it wasn't wearing its mask, and Vincent realized with a kind of numb horror that it wasn't a synthetic at all. He was struck speechless, his pleas dying in his throat, barely able to believe what he was seeing.

The creature that stared down at him was the ugliest, most alien-looking thing he'd ever seen—a giant, bony head, speckled and fleshy, four fingerlike pincers on its beady-eyed, pink-mouthed, noseless face, each tipped with a gleaming tusk.

"What are you," Vincent whispered, and the creature's pincers opened outward, fully exposing the small, pointed teeth in its strange mouth. The creature reached for something on its arm, holding its clawed hand up as it touched some kind of a bracelet—

—and Vincent heard his own voice spill out, "—no, no, don't wanna die, please—"

—and the creature flexed its arm, and two extremely sharp and nasty-looking blades sprang out from behind its hand, curved and shining in the firelight, and Vincent closed his eyes, thinking that if it was a bad dream, some hallucination, he wouldn't—

21

Ellis heard them calling his name and moved away as quietly as he could, deeply thankful that he hadn't killed them. They hadn't been hurt by the fall; Lara had a little bit of a limp but she'd told Jess it was nothing, and Jess hadn't been messed up any worse. After the beating he'd taken—

—because I didn't help—

—and nearly being immolated, Ellis was grateful that his stupidity hadn't cost Jess anything more. He wasn't going to do any more harm, to either of them—and that meant staying away. He was just lucky that he'd landed far enough from them that he'd had time to—

Ellis stumbled over a broken branch and froze, hoping that they hadn't heard. He was so clumsy, and he'd hit his head when he'd fallen, hard enough that his interface wound had started oozing again. He felt dizzy and strange, but in a way, his mind was clearer than it had been since before DS 949.

Max, if I could only get to Max and protect them, save them again like before . . .

Before. Stronger, smarter, *better*, seeing the dangers as glowing green shapes surrounded by lines, calculating distance and finding the optimum kill method in less time than it took to actually *think* it. The feelings he'd had then, so unimportant, so secondary to the task at hand. Ellis-Max, Max-Ellis, two as one, accomplishing such, such—unity. Perfection.

"Ellis? Can you hear me?" Lara called, far to his right. At least six or seven meters, maybe as much as 7.40 . . .

Ellis finally let himself move again, wondering how he could have let himself be alone for so long when Max was waiting. There was no decision to make. They had all landed close to the burning, dying station, but he'd already led them far enough away that he'd be able to circle back, to get to the shuttle and Max before they could stop him.

The thought that even trying to interface again could kill him didn't cross his mind. It was the kind of fear that Brian Ellis would have had.

For a time, there was darkness, interrupted by brief bursts of sensation. Movement, and a hissing sound. Something shiny and slender and hard against his chest. A jungle smell, and wetness seeping through his suit, a clammy gel against his skin.

It was the wetness that finally woke Briggs up, the cool feel of the syrupy liquid dragging his mind out of the dark. For a brief moment, he had absolutely no idea where he was or how he'd come to be there—too brief, because as his memory came flooding back, the realization of where he'd ended up came with it. Neither one was particularly pleasant.

Some Company competitor had blown the survey station apart, and he'd apparently been knocked unconscious when he'd fallen from the platform—and then taken, and now he was—well, surely he wouldn't actually be *injured* in any way, Nirasawa or Keene would come before anything could happen . . .

Briggs shifted uncomfortably, his back against a tree, a thick band of resinlike substance binding his arms to his sides and holding him up. In front of him was an egg. An alien egg.

Biotech, has to be. Their program isn't that far behind ours, they could have transported some individual drones to Bunda, waited until one transformed, started a new nest . . .

Yes, that was it. Biotech had sabotaged the survey station because—because it was Company, that was all they cared about, just some random selection of a rival's site for their own experiments. That it happened to be on Bunda, and that the survivors of DS 949 had landed here—coincidence. They'd sent in their new synthetic breed to obtain the 949 data, because they knew the planet had been infected; it made perfect sense now that he thought about it. They wouldn't want to risk lives when they had such marvelous new toys, invisible soldiers that could be tested against their XT nest . . .

Quite a coincidence, I'll have to get Nirasawa to calculate the odds on that when he—

Briggs heard a hissing from somewhere behind him and tensed, turning his head as far as he could to look for the source. No good. All he could see was the bark of the tree he'd been secured to, a pasty gray blur. Really, it was too dark to see much of anything. He couldn't be far from the station, he could smell the searing stench of burning plastics, but there wasn't any firelight. The only illumination came from the stars, a soft, pale light that gave his surroundings a dreamy, ethereal quality.

He looked at the egg again, smooth and unbroken, and felt the first sliver of real fear slip into his mind. What if . . .

"Ridiculous," he muttered, shifting uncomfortably. He was Lucas Briggs, upper six figures plus full WY perks, a palatial home in New Japan, only a fraction of a millimeter away from a spot on the Board. A spot that was as good as his, once he filed his report.

Positive thinking. Like what I'll do to that pilot, once we're off Bunda. Like the look on Julia Russ's face when she hears about my promotion.

Keene was probably still guarding the trio of prisoners, so it would be Nirasawa who found him; it was better that way. Keene was good but the synth would be able to handle a few drones with his bare hands. Much more efficient, much faster.

Briggs stared at the egg for a long moment, then cleared his throat, thinking that perhaps it would help things along if he made his position known.

"Nirasawa! I'm here!"

As if waiting for the sound of his voice, the top of the egg opened. Four thick, mucousy petals folded back, something moving in the shadowy center. Something pulsing, glistening in the faint bluish light cast down from above.

"Nirasawa!"

More hisses rose up around him, shadows moving out from the trees, but he couldn't look away from the egg. This was laughable, he was *Lucas Briggs*, this couldn't possibly be happening, *think positive, think positive—*

"NIRASAWA, KEENE, GET OVER HERE NOW!"

Like a spider, like some slick and impossible insect, the face-hugger leapt from its cold, unsealed womb. It was so fast that Briggs didn't have any more time to consider how very unlikely this outcome was, how things like this simply didn't happen to executives of his rank.

By the time Noguchi saw them, it was too late. The *Shell* had already touched the tops of the trees, roughly grinding through them, snapping them like twigs. Even strapped in, the ride was rough; she could hear the bodies in the dock being thrown against the walls, the ship alarms clattering and trilling that it was not a cleared landing zone, telling her that the *Shell* was suffering irreparable damage. As if she didn't know.

The ship continued its reckless half crash into the trees, the night broken by the reflected light of the giant, dying fire close by—and Noguchi saw the two humans in the viewscreen as the *Shell* actually touched the ground, a tremendous, dragging *crunch* of wood being forced into the soil, of plants and trees being chopped down by the nose of the still-moving ship.

No!

Noguchi saw the two figures running, pumping hell-bent to get out of the way—and then the ship plowed upward, the jerking image of the fleeing people gone from the screen. She saw shadowed green, moving, she saw a flash of dark sky, then green again—and then it was over, the *Shell* coming to rest.

The second she felt that the ship had settled, she popped the seat harness and grabbed her mask, desperate to get out, to see if she'd done the unthinkable. What a cruel irony it would be, to be responsible for killing people she'd come to save from the Hunters, a Clan ship the instrument of their deaths.

She doubted that the queen had survived the landing, but she hesitated at the hatch back into the shuttle dock all the same, listening. She'd already half slipped into battle mode, all of her senses tuning up for whatever came next. There was nothing but the clattering, hissing alarm, no sound, no *feel* of movement. Noguchi moved quickly across the dock, popping the air-lock door on the east side.

The rush of air seemed cold compared to the *Shell*'s heated atmosphere, and she welcomed it, breathing deeply as she looked down, assessing her climb. The ship was easily twenty-five meters high, but there were trees pressed against the side, less than a four-meter drop to the closest branch; Noguchi donned her mask and quickly lowered herself over the lock's edge, able to slide part of the way down the *Shell*'s curving slope.

From the trees to the ground it was an easy climb,

mostly dropping from branch to branch, steadying herself with one hand against the hull. Her ankle was still sore from her fight with Shorty, but the rest of her injuries seemed to have melted away. As soon as her feet touched, she took off her mask, hurrying around to the front of the ship.

Please, let them be here, let them be unhurt—

Noguchi stepped away from the ship, searching—and there they were, standing in a small semi-clearing right in front of the *Shell*. A man and a woman, both disheveled and dirty, both staring at her as if she were an alien; the thought made her smile, just a little. The woman, who held a handgun, lowered it slightly. They glanced at each other uncertainly, then back at her.

A sudden crunch of nerves hit her, seeing two human faces, human *expressions* for the first time in—

—three years, it's been three years. What must I look like, what are they thinking? What am I going to say?

Noguchi forced herself to relax. She'd tell them the truth, that was all.

The woman was slender, long, reddish hair framing an intelligent and wary face. The man was dark-skinned, of African descent perhaps, and had been hurt recently; bruises covered his face and one of his eyes was badly swollen. Only the woman was armed, though the male held himself carefully, obviously prepared to fight if she were an attacker.

Noguchi swallowed dryly, stepping closer to the couple. "Sorry," she said, still smiling just a little, her heart pounding as if she faced an army of drones. "I've never had much luck with landings. My name is Machiko Noguchi, and I'm here to help."

22

Of all the weird shit Jess had seen and experienced in the last couple of weeks, this had to be, hands down, the absolute mother of 'em all. The crash landing of a *giant* alien ship that had very nearly run them down, followed by the appearance of a small, deadly-looking Japanese woman, maybe early 30s TS, with beaded hair and a scar shaped like a lightning bolt between her eyes. Wearing alien armor that looked a hell of a lot like the armor on that cloaked creature . . .

. . . *and the hair, and that mask she's holding* . . .

"You're human," he said finally, a stupid statement but all he could think of; he wanted *reassurance.*

The woman, Noguchi, nodded almost shyly. "Yeah. Um, thanks. I—you'll have to excuse me, I haven't—you don't know how good it is to speak to people again."

They stood for a moment not speaking at all, just staring at one another, the crackling light of the ebbing station fire making it all seem even stranger, jagged shadows dancing across the peculiar scene. Jess knew that they had to find Ellis, that they needed weapons and supplies, that they had to get off of Bunda—but all he could do was stare at this woman, wondering when he was going to wake up.

And just when I thought things couldn't get any more fantastic. Christ, what a freak show.

Lara finally broke their odd silence, taking a step toward Noguchi. "You said you were here to help, Ms. Noguchi—do you mind telling us exactly what's going on?"

Her smile gone, Noguchi looked down at the mask in her hands before answering, her stilted voice gaining strength as she spoke. "It's kind of a long story. I heard that people on this planet—on Bunda—were in trouble, and I knew that I had to choose which side I was going to be on, the Hunters' or yours."

Jess frowned, making the connection between the woman's clothes and hair and the thing that had jumped him near the shuttle; apparently, there was more than one. "The Hunters? The invisible, uh, people who attacked the survey station? You're with them?"

"I've been with them for over a year," Noguchi said. "And they're not human. I thought—I learned the hard way that it was a mistake to think a human being could adapt to their culture. Their Clan."

She grinned, the look of it sending a chill down Jess's spine. He'd had a hard life, and didn't know that he'd ever seen anything as dangerous as that smile. "Now *they're* learning just how big a mistake it was."

Jesus, who is this woman?

Noguchi shook her head, as if clearing it. "Look, I made quite an entrance, so it won't be long before we have company. Are there any other survivors? We've got to round them up and get to cover."

Lara glanced over at him, and he shrugged, grimacing at the dozens of aches the action inspired. If there were any people left, the chances of finding them didn't seem so hot.

"You aren't the only ones, are you?" Noguchi asked.

"There are three of us, actually," Lara said. "There may be others, but . . . I guess we have a long story of our own."

Noguchi nodded, scanning the trees behind them with the practiced ease of someone used to battle while Lara spoke. "And I'm interested in hearing it, but we're going to need more weapons," she said. "Stay here."

Without waiting for a response, she turned and walked quickly back around the mammoth nose of the alien ship, disappearing through the dancing, smoking shadows that twined through the broken trees.

" 'Hunters?' " Lara said quietly. "What are they hunting?"

Jess shook his head. "Us. I don't know. Maybe she can help us find Ellis, at least . . ."

He trailed off, wondering if Lara had considered the possibility that the kid wasn't lying in the dirt somewhere, knocked out. The way he'd acted just before the platform crashed, guilt-ridden and near hysteria— maybe he'd run off, his fragile emotional state finally hitting overload.

Or could be he got killed by one of these alien friends of Ms. Noguchi's . . . The sudden appearance of the woman didn't seem real, even though the proof was right in front of them, twenty-plus meters high. Jess tried to think of something to say to Lara about the newest addition to their little party, feeling like they should have some exchange before she returned.

What's to say? She's here, and we're not in a position to turn away help, no matter how strange the helper.

"You think she's okay? Trustworthy?" Jess asked finally.

Lara hesitated for a second, then nodded. "Yeah. My gut says yeah."

Jess nodded, glad they agreed on her basic intentions if nothing else. Noguchi might be certifiable, but she obviously meant well.

Before they could talk any more, the woman reappeared, striding through the long grasses of the partial clearing. She held two riflelike weapons in addition to the one strapped to her back. They looked something like old-style machine guns with oversize grips.

"These are, uh, burners," she said, handing Jess one of the heavy weapons, the other to Lara. She unshouldered her own, holding it up for them to see the long, flat button on the front grip.

"Trigger. There's no safety, so be careful. No kick, either, but they ride high. They're kind of—they shoot a semiliquid pulse of . . . explosive particles, I guess. I've—I'm not much of a scientist, you'll have to forgive my lack of knowledge here . . ."

Jess held the ungainly "burner," remembering how big the creature that had attacked him had been; Noguchi handled hers easily, obviously comfortable with the overlong barrel and thick grips. Jess was suddenly extremely glad that she'd decided to show up; she was something else . . .

Noguchi cleared her throat, looking between the two of them, smiling nervously again. "I'm sorry, I haven't even asked your names."

Amazing. She crashes a ship, shows up talking about traveling with a pack of aliens, and still blushes when she talks.

Lara gripped the burner tightly, speaking calmly to the anxious woman. "I'm Katherine Lara, this is Martin Jess. The third member of our group is Brian Ellis; when the platform crashed, we lost track of him. As for any others . . . a private shuttle and I think a couple of transports got away before the station went down, so maybe they're already safe."

Jess nodded, realizing that Noguchi would need some background for their little saga to make sense. He picked the story up, trying to keep it short. "There are these creatures—aliens—that have been discovered all over the colonies. They're extremely dangerous, they can adapt to any environment, and they breed like nothing you've ever seen. Lara, Ellis, and I were part of an extermination team that was sent to a space station a little over a week ago, to wipe out a nest of them. What we didn't know was that the station had been deliberately infested . . ."

Jess hesitated, feeling the same old rage rising up. ". . . by the company we work for. They wanted to see how long it would take the aliens to kill four hundred people. *Families*."

He suddenly wished desperately that Briggs was still on Bunda, the rush of anger blocking out all other concerns. Lara touched his shoulder gently, taking over. "We lost two members of our ground team, and ended up here. They sent a suit—an executive—to see if we had the information about the nest spread, but we don't, it got blown up along with the station and about a thousand aliens. Bugs, we call them—"

Noguchi had listened to them without expression, but now she nodded, apparently unsurprised by their story—and what she said next was a shock that reminded Jess of his earlier idiotic assumption, that meeting this woman was the strangest thing that had happened, that *could* happen.

"I call them that, too. We have more in common than you know. To the Clan, they are *kainde amedha*, the Hard Meat. They are what the Hunters usually Hunt—and this world has been seeded with them."

Lara and Jess wore twin expressions of astonishment. Noguchi found herself marveling at the look of them both, at the intricate, telling lines and planes of their faces. If yautja faces were capable of subtlety, she'd never seen it.

Finish talking, there can't be much time left.

"There was even a bug mother on our ship," she said, nodding toward the grounded *Shell*. "Probably dead now. The Hunters seed entire planets with eggs and Hunt drones for sport. It's—their entire culture is built around the Hunt, it's very much like a religion for them."

Noguchi sighed, shaking her head. "I thought they had rules against Hunting intelligent life. Against Hunting humans. It seems I was wrong."

Lara stared at her. "You mean they hunt bugs for *fun*?"

Noguchi nodded. "Apparently they started their Hunt in another part of Bunda, but it's still early. They'll be heading this way very soon. You haven't seen any bugs yet?"

They both shook their heads, and she was glad to note that both immediately started watching the dark walls of jungle, alert to new danger. That they had been part of an extermination crew was good, they wouldn't be entirely helpless against the drones, at least . . .

"What about your friend, Ellis?" Noguchi asked. "You say you lost him?"

Lara nodded, but Jess shifted uncomfortably, his bruised face set unhappily.

"He may have lost us," he said softly. Noguchi noticed that Lara didn't seem surprised by the differing opinion, even though it was obvious they hadn't discussed it.

"Another long story, but let's just say that he was injured on that space station, got kinda fucked up," Jess went on. "I think maybe he took off after the platform went down. He thought it was his fault."

Noguchi wasn't sure what to make of that. She hoped that they found him before any of the Hunters did—

—except that it was already too late. The tiniest whiff of yautja musk was in the burnt air, she caught it even as she heard the soft *snap* of a branch underfoot, some twenty meters away, a slight rustling of leaves not far from it.

Novices, and they won't be alone.

"Get behind me, now," she said, putting the mask

on, wondering how many had come. It was a Blooding
Hunt, only a few should have burners—except it had
been a human Hunt, too, no way to know how heavily
they'd armed themselves, she hadn't checked the
weapon stock . . .

     . . . *and it doesn't matter, I have to protect them, get
them out of harm's way* . . .

Noguchi backed away from the line of trees, back
toward the ship, Jess and Lara flanking her, covering
either side. The Hunters wouldn't attack from a distance—although she couldn't be positive, not knowing
what rules they followed for Hunting ooman—

—*no, human. Human beings. Kate Lara and Martin
Jess.*

After so long with the Hunters, she was astounded
at how quickly she'd warmed to these two, and how
easily they'd accepted her. These weren't the simpering
colonists or corporate flunkies she'd expected; she
would have fought for them either way, but the fact
that they hunted bugs, that they were warriors of a
sort, more than made up for the fact that she was risking her life to save only two people. These were *her*
people.

Noguchi knew that she was as swift and sure as any
one of the Hunters, not as strong but undoubtedly
smarter—because she wasn't so arrogant as to believe
she would always prevail.

*And I might lose . . . but I'll be damned if I die with-
out taking some of them with me.*

She'd get these people to safety, and then finish
her business with the Hunters. As soon as they made it
into the deep shadow of the broken ship, Noguchi
turned and ran, Lara and Ellis close behind as they
plunged into the night jungle.

23

Noguchi ran through the dark scrub as though she were dancing, dodging branches and leaping over fallen trees with the grace and stamina of an expert gymnast—and she did it almost silently, making Lara wonder if the woman were a synthetic. She and Jess could barely keep up, and between them, they made enough noise to alert the dead.

What did she hear, where are we going, how the hell are we going to hold our own against a race of bug hunters?

The questions whipped through her mind, unanswerable, everything happening too fast. There was a growing ache in her right knee that got a little worse with each running step, making her wonder just how bad she'd screwed it up when the platform had gone down—and though they were veering away from the burning rubble of the station, smoke-thick, ambient light still layered through the trees, enough for her to see that Jess wasn't doing so great, either. She clutched the heavy weapon against her chest and struggled on, darting looks back at Jess to make sure he was still with them.

Just as Lara thought she might have to fall back, Noguchi slowed, holding up one gloved hand. The smaller woman raised her burner, cocking her head as if listening for something. Lara couldn't hear anything over the rapid thumps of her own heart, and Jess was trying not to gasp without much success.

This is crazy and we left Ellis behind, we have to—

Lara froze, hearing the hiss, the sweat on her skin turning cold. She raised her own weapon, darting a look back to see that Jess had also heard. The rising, breathing hiss of a drone or drones, close, nearly impossible to pinpoint—

—and Noguchi fired, the burner making a *brrrp* sound, a strobe of brilliant blue-white exploding through the hanging branches and vines, BOOM! Plant matter flew, and Lara heard the shriek of a second bug even as the first was finally visible, making itself seen in bloody death. Noguchi's shot had blown through the drone's midsection, cutting it in two, both pieces crashing through the shadowed green on a spray of acid.

Before Lara or Jess could find the second screamer, Noguchi fired again, just to the right of the first. Again, they saw the drone as it died, the bug's scream shattering out the back of its black skull. Leaves smoked and sizzled, a fresh smell of burning in the already soured air.

Didn't even see them—

Lara heard another alien trumpet, and another, ahead of them and at two o'clock. The bugs weren't close enough to attack, not yet, but the jungle was suddenly alive with crashing movement, with the approach of many.

"*Nest,*" Jess spat, and Lara knew it was true, knew that there wouldn't be such a deliberate attack unless they were near a breeding area.

Noguchi knew it, too. "Turn around," she said, her voice hollow from beneath her alien mask. She swept the trees with her burner, backing away from the hissing, the popping snaps of branches, from the distant shrieks growing by the second.

Lara turned, stepping in front of Jess and moving quickly back the way they'd come. She could hear Jess's ragged breathing behind her as she jumped a huddle of stocky plants, and from farther back, the ripping sound of Noguchi's burner as it fired again.

Back to that ship, maybe the damage isn't so bad and we can—

To Lara's left, a bug lunged out from behind a stand of trees, grinning and hissing, its clawed hands snatching. Lara stumbled as she brought the awkward rifle around, fumbling for the trigger—

—and *brrrp-BOOM*, a bolt of lightning tore through the air from behind her, from Jess's weapon, melting through the alien's spindly body, its left side disappearing in a liquid splash.

They didn't have time to stop, to regroup; if they didn't get out of the designated no-man's-land, the drones would keep coming. Lara glanced back, saw that Jess was on his feet, and sprinted ahead. She had no doubt that Noguchi was still bringing up the rear, not with how fast she'd wasted those first two—

"Stop!" Noguchi hissed, and Lara stumbled to a halt, every muscle in her body telling her to run, her soldier's mind obeying the voice of command—and a strange smell washed over her, like some rotting, oily fruit.

"Toward the station, go!" Noguchi said.

Lara turned right and saw Jess already a step ahead. Together they ran toward the glow of the fire, and it occurred to Lara that in a matter of minutes, they had accepted the unusual woman as their leader—and maybe as their only real chance to get off of Bunda alive.

The shuttle had landed on its side at an angle, the few things that had been aboard spilling out of the open hatch—including Keene's body, his dark suit smeared with the contents of a few food packets, a spongy chunk of soypro actually stuck to one of his glazed, bulging eyes. Only his upper half was outside, his chest crushed between the doorframe and the ground, gluts of drying blood coming from every visible orifice. Ellis barely noticed, interested only in Max's condition as he crawled over the corpse's legs, searching the shadows beneath the webbed cots that hung down from what was now the ceiling. He stood up in the stifling dark, everything that had happened in the past hours jumbling together, focusing his energy on the joining to come.

They need us now, they need what we can do.

There had been a terrible crash, an alien ship twice as big as the *Nemesis* plowing through the trees, almost hitting Lara and Jess. Ellis had just reached the shuttle, their crashed transport close enough to the fire that one side was smoking, when he'd seen the ship come down. He'd had to run back, to make sure they hadn't been killed. A glimpse through the trees, the two of them standing in front of the ship, and the relief that had flowed through him had been incredible—not just because they were still alive, but because he still had a real reason to interface again with Max. As long as they were alive on this dangerous planet, they needed what he and Max had to offer.

It's who I am now. I thought I was sick, I thought the numbers and nonfeelings were a sickness, but they weren't. They aren't.

"They're us," Ellis breathed, talking to the thickening of shadow in the back of the transport. His glasses had been lost, he couldn't remember when, but it was okay. Max would see for them both.

He felt his way through the dark, falling to his knees and crawling when he tripped over something, reaching out to touch Max. The heated air made the metal warm, as though Max had been waiting, warming its empty guts for Ellis to slip inside.

Max was on its left side, its rifle arm pinned beneath its giant torso. Ellis crawled over the metal body, feeling for the circuit hatch set at the lower back. He found it and found the controls that would ready Max, his hands knowing what to do even without the years of training in hydraulic chem or the Company course; this was Max, as much a part of him now as he was of it. He stroked the chords that would sing it to life, grinning with excitement as he turned on the vocal transmit option, no headsets here, *and they'll hear my voice, mine, speaking for us as we lead them to safety* . . .

Next, the release on its back panel. With a silent plea, Ellis twisted the lock for the cavity.

Yes! It hadn't been jammed. Metal slid against metal, the hatch rising, stopping short of its full length when it hit the back wall. There was just enough room for him to slip inside.

Ellis wormed his way into the suit, wishing absently that he'd thought to look over Max's condition when they'd still been drifting in the void. Before they'd joined on the station, he'd only had a moment to make adjustments—resetting the interface arm at the back of the head, switching off the IV pumps and monitors, doing all he could so that they could work together without a comp-synth implant. Toward the end of their time together, when his body had started to—

—die—

—rebel against Max, he'd had to randomly shut down some of the systems. It had been a blind and desperate act, but it had worked, giving him enough control over Max for them to make it off the station. He knew now, though, that it had been such a struggle, his body failing as it had *because* he'd worked to dominate the machine.

"Not again," he said, working his legs into Max's, his feet finding the stirrups set just above the suit's knees. He reached back and closed the hatch, the interior's temp jumping several degrees, from hot to suffocating. Once Max was awake, the cooling system would kick on . . .

Ellis pressed his arms to his sides, finding the touch-sensitive controls with his fingers, breathing deeply. Old sweat, chemicals, burnt wiring—smells that instantly took him back, the disjointed memories rising close to the surface. There was another scent, uglier, and he remembered that he'd vomited near the end—

—blood, you threw up blood—

—but he knew his olfactory senses would pretty much shut down once Max took over. All that was left was to lean back. The interface probe would complete the process when it touched him.

Ellis closed his eyes, preparing himself for the initial pain as best he could; he took a deep breath and pushed his head back, a slight smile on his face as he felt the metal tip of the longer spike, as he heard the probe hum into action—

—and the pain was so sudden, so complete that for a half second, he was Brian Ellis again, a person, his thoughts all his own—and he knew that he'd made a horrible mistake, and that it was too late as his limbs started to convulse, as the prongs worked their way into him, boring the old holes wider, his blood spurting into the hot black of the robotic suit.

Nirasawa had been damaged, parts of his program inaccessible, parts of his body in need of repair, but he put these matters aside; Mr. Briggs had been taken away. Mr. Briggs could very well be in danger, and Nirasawa would deal with his own problems once he'd found and secured the safety of Mr. Briggs.

It had been nearly twenty-four minutes since he'd last seen Mr. Briggs, on the second northwest deck of the Bunda survey station. The being that Nirasawa had been working to restrain had not been killed when the station had fallen, and Nirasawa had been detained from his primary function by the being once on the ground. The being, alien/organic in nature, had been injured, making it easier for Nirasawa to render it harmless; he'd broken all four limbs and thrown its weapon away. The being had died within seven minutes, although Nirasawa could not be any more specific as to the exact time; he'd already begun a perimeter search for Mr. Briggs, and had passed the dead alien being seven minutes after he'd initially left it. The being could have ceased living at any period during those minutes.

Mr. Briggs had chosen not to be implanted with a signal 07901 patch, compatible to all Cyberdyne 07901 Guard series. Mr. Briggs's position would be known to Nirasawa at all times if Mr. Briggs had been implanted. It was a simple procedure, a painless injection that fulfilled all terms of Nirasawa's warranty and would ensure a higher level of satisfaction on the part of Mr. Briggs; Nirasawa found it unfortunate that Mr. Briggs had declined the patch. Since he had no signal input, Nirasawa would have to search as programmed, an expanding perimeter search with possible directional changes based on suggestive evidence found.

Nirasawa's search had been unsuccessful. The station's malfunction and subsequent crash had created the problem of too much suggestive evidence, so Nirasawa had found it necessary to reduce his dependence on his heuristic logic driver, relying primarily on his intuitive functions. This, unfortunately, was one of the areas that had suffered damage, between 300 and 330 of the self-mapping connective loops no longer functioning. Nirasawa could not narrow the number down any further. He continued his expansion, temporarily reducing power to damaged areas as he walked, searching for Mr. Briggs. He did not call for him, the existence of hostile beings making vocal contact a risk in the possible instance that Mr. Briggs was being held.

Nirasawa found Mr. Briggs fifty-two meters from the outer edge of the defunct station, thirty-three minutes since last contact, Mr. Briggs restrained by an organic substance that bound him to the trunk of a large tree. Nirasawa sensed that there were several hidden beings in the vicinity but there were no threatening movements, so he did not increase their priority status. There was an alien ovoid in front of Mr. Briggs, and an alien body attached to Mr. Briggs's face.

Nirasawa acted quickly to fulfill his primary function. He began to pull the foreign body from Mr. Briggs's face—and immediately, Mr. Briggs began to choke, the being's multiple legs tightening in a possibly damaging way around Mr. Briggs's head. Nirasawa ceased his efforts. There was a possibility that he knew what to do, that he understood what the alien body was, but that he'd lost access to that part of his program. As it was, he did not know how to protect Mr. Briggs from this threat.

Nirasawa saw that there were several animals similarly restrained in the immediate area, small mammals, many of them dead. All of them also had alien ovoids in front of them. Eggs. The probability that Mr. Briggs would die increased sharply with this information, and Nirasawa decided that it would be best to remove him from the situation.

Nirasawa carefully broke the stiff substance away from Mr. Briggs and lifted him, walking away from the egg area. He'd heard sounds of deliberate, high-functioning movement just after the alien craft had set down, eleven minutes earlier. If there were humans still on Bunda, perhaps he could seek out repair, for himself and for Mr. Briggs. It certainly couldn't hurt.

24

The decision was instantaneous, Noguchi calling out to Lara and Jess with the same breath that had inhaled the yautja musk. The Hunters probably knew it was she, and it occurred to her in that same instant that the recognition might inspire a different kind of Hunt. She had to separate from Lara and Jess; being marked as Noguchi's friends certainly wouldn't buy them any favor. Besides which, she'd led the trusting pair from the arms of the Hunters into the dangers of a bug zone and back again; she couldn't have known about the bugs, but she was responsible for what happened next, having taken it upon herself to step into a leadership role.

As soon as she shouted them toward the dying light of the station fire, she veered left, running in the opposite direction. If the Hunters went after Lara and Jess, the fire should confuse their infra sensors—the reason they even *had* infra finally clear—but chances were good that they'd be coming after her first.

There's no enemy like an old enemy, after all . . .

An ordinary human trophy would be nothing next

to her skull on one of their walls; any Blooded worth his mark would have made the connection between the crashed ship and her running with humans, the magnitude of the betrayal such that they might very well leave off the Hunt, calling for her extermination over all else. She'd known that they would want her dead, but it hadn't figured that prominently in her plans—she hadn't known that she would be working to save only two people, that there would be so few targets for the Hunters' hatred. It probably couldn't be helped, but she had to at least try and redirect their attention.

Lead them toward the bugs, circle back for Lara and Jess and see if we can't find Topknot's ship. If she'd read the signal right back on the *Shell*, his transport was only about a klick and a half west from her current—

Brrrp—

—*BOOM*, Noguchi was already diving, rolling through a tangle of bushes as a rain of fiery leaves fell all around her. She was on her feet and running again before they finished dropping, zagging right. The alien grounds were close, she should be drawing attack any second. Drones sometimes gathered unhatched eggs on seeded planets, protecting them fiercely; it was a bad place to lead novice Hunters, dangerous, and if those chasing her now didn't break off their pursuit, they were going to have more to deal with than a single renegade ooman—

—and *there*, coiling out of the dark like a bone ghost, a leering, lashing drone, hopping into her path from any one of a hundred places. Noguchi dodged left, pivoting, throwing herself back against a willowy tree as she brought up her burner. She fired, the blast catching the bug's shoulder, spinning it away—

—and she heard the clattering, trilling cry of a Hunter, a Leader, a howl joined by five, seven, ten others, more. If they hadn't recognized her before, any question was now gone—and she'd given them their target, killing without instruction in front of a Leader and his group. The rising cries grew in ferocity, a harmony of bloodlust that she'd once participated in, the one experience she'd shared with the predatory Clan, that she'd understood. The fevered, soul-consuming joy of Hunt—and this time, she was their prey.

But not an easy kill, her thoughts reaffirmed. *They want a fight, they've got it.*

Noguchi slipped around the tree and was away, the howl of the Hunters met by the screams of approaching drones, the two blending into a hellish music that spun up into the darkness, a melody of war.

Parts of the station fire had died to embers, chemical smoke and heat but no flame. Jess and Lara moved as far as they could into the mass of debris, the wreckage seeming to stretch forever. They'd found a large, jutting piece of blackened deck to stand behind, shielded from the open jungle—but it was too hot to lean against, and as the moments ticked past, Noguchi nowhere to be seen, Jess felt his energy failing. They heard animal sounds, screams, bugs and something else from somewhere not far away, but he couldn't find the desire to care. He blinked, rubbing at his burning eyes—

—and suddenly, Lara was supporting him, holding him up, Jess fighting off a wave of vertigo and nausea.

"Jess? Are you okay?"

He let himself lean on her as much as he thought he could, smiling wearily at the look of worry on her smudged face. A couple of weeks ago, she'd been his boss, contracted Company on the H/K Max team he'd been serving time on. Hard to believe how much had changed—and he felt a sudden rush of love for her that was entirely pure, a feeling of connection that had nothing to do with sex or power or their positions in life. This woman, this *person*, had backed him up when things were bad, and continued to do so, because of who she was.

Me, too, Lara. As long as I'm able, you got what I have . . .

There weren't enough good words to express such a depth of camaraderie—and besides, it was cornball. He shook his head, thinking that human beings surely were a messed-up bunch; it was no wonder Noguchi had opted to fly away with a bunch of aliens.

"I'll survive," he said, then grinned. "Then, it isn't really up to me, is it?"

Lara grinned back, opening her mouth to reply—

—and they heard Noguchi's voice less than a meter away, startling both of them. "Were either of you hurt?"

She stepped around the hunk of burnt deck as noiselessly as she'd approached, removing her mask as both of them shook their heads, Jess wondering again who the hell this woman *was*.

"I'm sorry, I ran into a Hunting group," she said. "I led them back toward the drones, but I don't know if they engaged; we'll have to steer clear of both, hope for the best." Her lightly sweating face was as calm as if she'd just told them what the weather was like.

"The Leader—one of the Hunters has a ship, maybe two kilometers that way," Noguchi went on, pointing west. "It won't be guarded . . ."

She trailed off, and Jess realized that she was studying him, her sharp gaze taking in his stance and the bruises on his face. "Will you be able to walk?"

He didn't give her a knee-jerk response, realizing that a macho "yeah, of course," while good for his ego, wasn't going to help all that much if he collapsed in the jungle.

Jess took a deep breath, feeling the aches from Keene's beating, from the run-in with the Hunter, from the station's crash—and nodded, knowing that he could go on.

"I'm good. Not for long, maybe, but I'm still good," he said.

Noguchi watched him a moment longer, then nodded, slipping her mask back on. "We'll pass back by where your friend was lost, then on to the ship. Stay close to me, both of you.''

Jess and Lara exchanged a look of understanding at her words, of mutual unhappiness and a reluctant acceptance. By unspoken agreement, they hadn't talked about the kid, about what they were going to do if they couldn't find him, but Noguchi had just said it for them. If they couldn't find Ellis, they'd have to leave him behind.

We'll find him. And if we don't, we can come back, do flybys until the sun's up, we're sure to see him . . . He held on to the thought, promising himself that they wouldn't leave Bunda without Ellis. Or Ellis's body.

Following Noguchi, they moved out from behind the broken deck, stepping carefully through the smoking pieces of the station, heading back toward the deeply shaded jungle. And then Jess heard something he'd heard before, in his nightmares and in the field, and felt his gut clench, felt his hopes for all of them dwindle to nothing. A monstrous shriek of animal fury, of hatred, of power and darkness, spilling out of the trees and enveloping them.

Queen.

The bug mother stepped out into the open from their left and screamed again, and at the sound of her terrible voice there was a crashing through the brush all around, hisses and trumpeting calls, her sleek children coming to join her.

As one, they raised their weapons—and heard and saw a band of giants glide out of the dark to their right, armored and masked, Noguchi's Hunters. Most held bladed staffs and all stood as warriors, silent and faceless, watching the trio of humans and giving nothing away.

For a beat, nothing moved. It was just enough time for Jess to take aim, and then everything exploded at once.

•   •   •

Brrrp-BOOM, Lara felt the burner heave up in her hands, the shot hitting a drone in front of the queen, the blast echoed by Jess and then Noguchi as they fired—

—*oh fuck what a mess*—

—and they were falling back, Lara firing again, swinging the weapon over to the charging Hunters, the bugs shrieking, Noguchi screaming words she couldn't hear. Noguchi's alien soldiers had flown into the group of drones, stabbing and howling, at least two of them firing burners of their own.

Lara stumbled, firing, hitting another of the bugs as it threw itself in front of its queen, dozens of drones pouring out of the jungle like a plague, surrounding their mother and lunging for both the Hunters and their own tiny group.

Noguchi spun and fired, fired, the strobing explosions of her burner taking out bug and Hunter alike. Jess shouted something and a blast from a Hunter's weapon blew past Lara close enough for her to feel its heat, deck shrapnel slapping at her lower back from the explosion. Lara swung her burner, found the warrior, and watched its masked head fly apart, the huge body hesitating headless in the air before crumpling—

—and another Hunter was scooping up the burner, firing it in their direction as a drone flew at him, clawing him to the ground, its grinning skull jaws tearing into his hidden flesh.

The queen continued her bursts of screams, all but hidden by a mass of her minions, bugs jumping into battle as more came out of the dark, running at the Hunters, the Hunters dancing and cutting like samurai—and both alien groups slowly, steadily, gaining ground on the three humans.

Lara didn't think about it, couldn't, aiming and firing and aiming again, the bugs blasted into acid-splash as the Hunters dodged and fought and somehow managed not to die—

—*CLICK CLICK CLICK*—

—and Lara heard Noguchi's weapon go dry, even over the screams and explosions, the sound as chilling and terrible as the queen's fury. Lara stepped forward, jabbing her burner at Noguchi as the woman dropped the dead one, taking hers—

—and in the half second that Noguchi wasn't firing, the tide of the slaughter drew closer. Lara fumbled for her handgun, *not enough, they'll all go dry, we're dead.*

They continued to back away but there was no denying that it was a matter of minutes, seconds before they were overrun. To turn and flee was certain death, by burner or by bug, and Lara found a Hunter's masked face and fired, the *bam bam bam* of the semi adding a tempo to the bloody battle, firing because it was that or give up—

—and suddenly, so suddenly that Lara didn't understand for a moment what was happening, Hunters and drones alike began to collapse, the sound of rapid fire dull thunder to her ringing ears. There was a stuttering light washing across the falling bodies, across all of them. It was the muzzle flash of a pulse rifle, M41 or '56, and Lara's uncomprehending gaze followed the flashing bursts to their source, to their right and behind—

—and saw Max. Standing in the midst of the ocean of debris, small fires licking at the suit's giant legs, bright tongues against the matte orange of its armored body.

Max took a step toward them, still firing, one mighty, quad-tread foot crunching down through a layer of broken station, its left arm sending a constant stream of armor-piercing death into the fray.

"Ellis," she whispered, the sound lost in the rain of bullets and the queen's screaming retreat, her brood swarming around her like a living veil. The Hunters, too, melted back into the jungle, leaving their fallen behind, the crush of bodies smoking from the wash of drone blood.

Max continued to fire and Lara felt Jess's hand on

her arm, pulling at her, dragging her back behind their shield of docking where Noguchi stood, her calm finally broken; she'd removed her mask and stared wide-eyed at the monster robot that had stepped into the alien war, not understanding.

They'd found their friend. They'd found Ellis, and Noguchi didn't know yet what the interface meant for the man inside, but Lara felt a wrenching sadness sweep over her. Ellis was with Max again.

25

There were fourteen drones and a single queen, nine unidentified life-forms and three humans. Max calculated the distance between all of them and chose pulse over fire, Ellis struggling to translate the difference in the glowing green forms. Max had been designed to find an implant signal in the designated—

—Teape he was the designated—

—life-form and cut out firing before extermination could occur, destroying everything in its single-minded path to the beacon. These humans had no implants, and Max's mind had no signal urging it on. It was up to Ellis to manipulate the program, and his influence wasn't constant, his consciousness unstable; there was distant pain, distant understanding of body, radical fluctuations in awareness. Max did not know what these things meant, and it was all Ellis could do to hold on.

Max fired, sweeping in a contained pattern across the twenty-four alien objects that clustered in front of its sensors, closest at 17.3 meters, secondary liquid expulsion maximum two meters—

—*acid spray at its worst, can't let it reach the three forms because*—

Because Ellis realized that this was what had been designated, what he had wanted at some prior instance, *these are Lara and Jess and*. He pushed into the realm of sensory feed, his mind reaching for the stats and commands, finding them easily. Getting them to Max was harder, Ellis's elastic, human thoughts complicating the process.

Separate objects at 7. 7.3 8.4 active/cease.

Max continued to fire, the direction correlated, and Ellis was pleased—until a wave of dark slid through him, temporarily removing him from the whole. After some indeterminate time, he was with Max again. With Max's help, he estimated the loss of awareness to be no more than two seconds and no less than one.

Body mind is reacting, must not fight it but stay here, stay with Max. Max wouldn't work without him but he knew that he was being drained, that some vital part of Ellis was being used up. This was unavoidable, he accepted it—but he couldn't let the loss stop them from their purpose, and he didn't know how long he could go on.

The area had been cleared of all but the three objects he'd activated the cutoff for; Max continued to fire into the lines of the jungle, its sensors finding the forms of four figures previously identified as the not-drones—

—*like that one on the deck, they're hiding, watching, preparing. Badguys.*

Max accepted the identification. It sent thirty-two more rounds through the walls of shifting green, three of the badguys falling, the fourth retreating out of sensory range. Max discontinued its strike, waiting, not prepared to move without some input from Ellis.

One of the humans approached. Ellis struggled to the surface, wanting to be there for the interaction, needing to be; Max would not respond.

ellis, ellis are you

He pushed harder, the pain sharpening, becoming unpleasant. He pushed anyway, knowing that he recognized the voice, the cool and soothing voice that he had known many times before. He heard her, and heard the others speaking at the same time behind her, their voices softer. Max sorted through each vocal pattern and fed Ellis all three simultaneously, Ellis working through them as quickly as he could.

"Ellis? Brian? Can you speak? It's Lara, it's Katherine Lara—"

Lara!

"Your friend is inside a robot?" Small female, unknown.

"Not a robot. That's a MAX, Mobile Assault Exo-Warrior." *Stupid kid, I can't believe he'd do this to himself.* Jess, angry and worried, faded out like a wave in the abyss.

Lara, Ellis said or thought, he knew he should say more but couldn't find the strength. The darkness tried to take over again, but he held on, Lara was speaking and he wanted very much to tell her that he was okay, that it wasn't a mistake.

we're going to help you don't worry it's okay, brian, we'll get you out of there now

No. She didn't understand.

With a supreme force of will, Ellis found his voice. It was as distant and meaningless as his body, but he bent it to his will, meaning to make them understand. Max didn't understand, but Ellis had discovered that Max didn't necessarily need to understand everything.

"If you—survive you need me no argument Lara, Jess."

The trio of shapes held still, silent, and Ellis wasn't sure if they'd heard him, even as Max told him that his voice had registered in an audible range. It was Jess who spoke finally, and Ellis knew that he was trying not to cry. Max knew that the object was 1.1 meters distant.

"Okay, kid. This is Machiko Noguchi, she's a friend now. We're going to follow her to a ship and go home, so just hang on for a while, okay? We're going home."

Max requested data. Ellis explained that there was to be movement, the sound of words outside becoming sounds, Ellis moving back again so that Max could be strong for all of them.

Noguchi was glad that Lara and Jess agreed to their friend's decision, whether or not it was wisest for his health. The queen had escaped the *Shell*, she'd seen the link of chain still hanging from her ebony headdress, and knew now that she'd been a fool to believe that a simple crash could kill the bug mother.

And does she recognize me as the Hunters did? As the being who trapped her? No one knew enough about the species to say what a queen could or couldn't do, but she was surely smart enough. And if the queen actually understood who she was, it meant Noguchi was marked by two alien species as enemy, which meant that having the MAX with them bolstered their chances from none to slim.

And if I wasn't here at all, what would the chances be then?

Lara stood next to the MAX, looking up into the squared face of the suit, the smoking glow from the station fire softening the robot's sharp angles. It was easily three, three and a half meters tall and a meter across at its widest, humanoid, the numbers 09 in scuffed white on its thickly plated torso. It looked like a bodybuilder made from giant metal blocks, indestructible—but the look on Lara's face suggested that the man inside was anything but.

"The suit's constructed to interface with a surgical implant," Jess said softly. He'd hung back, standing with Noguchi near the crushed deck where they'd found cover. "Ellis doesn't have one. He went into Max back on that station, saved our lives, but it almost killed him."

Jess shook his head, a mix of sadness and respect in his deep, exhausted voice. "We should have known. Lara and I, we thought he was just sick, recovering, you know? But it seems like he got it in his head that this was all he could do to help."

Noguchi nodded slowly, feeling some small connection to Ellis, thinking that bravery and stupidity were often closely linked. *Like me, coming here, so fired up to break with the Hunters and avenge my honor that I didn't even consider what my presence could mean to these people.* At least Ellis had only risked himself; she'd risked all of them.

Noguchi walked toward Lara and "Max," Jess following. They needed to talk. When they were all together, she took a deep breath and dived in.

"The Hunters want my head," she said. "If they haven't already called off their Hunt to search for me, they're doing it now. The good thing is, they have rules, and I've been with them long enough to have some idea of what they are—but the queen doesn't, and she may want me even worse than they do. I think if we split up, meet at the transport—"

Lara cut her off, frowning sharply. "No. We stick together."

"They don't *want* you," Noguchi said patiently. "And you've got—Ellis to help you get to the ship. Two klicks west, that's the last signal reading—one of you has pilot training, right?"

Lara nodded. "Yes, but I don't—"

"The controls are intuitive," Noguchi said. "Except you push on the collective to gain altitude, and pull back to descend. I can't explain the navigational system, but you'll be able to get a safe distance away if I don't make it."

"No offense, but that's bullshit," Jess said angrily. "We're not splitting up, okay? You risked your life to get here, to get to us—"

"—and you're willing to risk yours to return the favor?" Noguchi snapped.

Jess and Lara were both silent for a beat, Ellis-Max standing mute and unmoving, only the hissing pops of the ebbing fire to be heard—and then Jess grinned, a tired, sweet smile.

"Well, yeah. Pretty much," he said, and Lara nodded.

Noguchi wanted to protest, but realized that they'd decided—and that in their position, she would do the same. The realization didn't lessen the feelings of warmth and gratitude that filled her; whatever happened, she knew now that she'd made the right choice.

My own kind.

"Let's go, then," she said, slipping on her mask and turning away, relieved that she could cover her face. She wasn't ashamed of her tears, but now wasn't the time for emotion; if these good people meant to stay with her, they were going to have to be ready for anything.

They moved into the wooded jungle, Noguchi in the lead, Ellis bringing up the rear. Jess stumbled along behind Lara, aching and bone weary, but with enough determination to hold himself together. Finding Ellis—or Ellis finding them—had provided Jess with another reason to keep going; he owed Ellis, and the kid had put his life on the line to help them. Again.

We gotta get him out of Max, ASAP. For as shitty as I feel, I didn't lobotomize myself. And if he could do that for us, I can at least get my sorry ass through a couple klicks of jungle.

They walked in silence, or as much as they could manage with a ton-plus of metal stomping behind them. The going wasn't too bad, although there was a lot of climbing over rotting logs and skirting trees, slowing them up. It would have been easier to let Max go first, clear them a path, but Lara had pointed out that he'd be more effective, better able to sense movement to either side, if he stayed in back. Ellis seemed to understand, although he'd said nothing when they'd explained it to them. Jess was afraid for him—the fear mixed with guilt, that they hadn't pulled him out of Max immediately.

He's right, though, we need him . . . The Hunters had been something to see, and Jess didn't know that defeating an alien queen was even possible without the kind of firepower Max possessed.

They'd just reached a clearing, a grassy area that Noguchi started to edge around, when Ellis stopped, the rumbling crunch of his steps cut off. They all froze, Jess feeling new fear for the kid, wondering if this was it, not even halfway to the alien transport. Ellis's weak, stuttering voice let Jess breathe again, but inspired a different kind of fear.

"Sssomeone coming," Ellis said, and raised both arms, aiming one o'clock.

Noguchi had already dropped into a crouch, weapon ready, and Jess and Lara followed suit, new adrenaline humming through his body as thoughts raced through his mind.

Hunter or drone, how many burner shots can Max take? The suit's solid but it wasn't built for those and what if this is a distraction, a trap—

Jess clamped down, had to keep his shit wired. He held the burner and waited. Noguchi held one of her hands up in a fist and twisted it back and forth; Jess didn't know the signal, but she seemed to realize that, whispering back at them a second later.

"Get ready."

A crashing, rustling sound, whatever it was getting closer, coming through the trees from across the small clearing. It was big, *could be anything*—

The shadowy figure stepped out into the starlight a second later and Jess almost fired, there was something wrong with it, the shape of its head strange, its torso deformed—

"Oh, God," Lara whispered, and Jess saw what it was, and felt a kind of vindication rise up inside, feelings of gratification that he recognized as petty and mean. And deeply satisfying.

It was Nirasawa, his face mutilated, the now obvious synthetic skin hanging in melted shreds from an exposed carbon-fiber cheekbone. And he was carrying Lucas Briggs, the exec's limp body in his arms, a facehugger wrapped tightly around the bastard's head.

26

"Don't shoot," Nirasawa said, a thick, wet quality to his voice, as if he were speaking through a mouthful of soup. He stepped toward them, holding out Briggs's body as if it were some token of surrender. What was left of the synthetic's face was held in an expression of unhappiness, almost sorrow.

An android. Thank God Keene wasn't, we never would have made it off that shuttle . . .

Lara shook her head. Considering where they were now, what Ellis had done to himself, maybe she shouldn't be so thankful.

Nirasawa came closer and Lara stood up, Jess and Noguchi following suit, though neither of them lowered their weapons. Lara tucked hers into her belt, stepping toward the damaged android. Ellis was the robotics expert, but she knew enough about synth programming to know that it was unlikely this was some trick. Synthetics didn't generally work that way, they had to be directed to be misleading, and it was obvious that Briggs wasn't capable of redesigning a program, not at the moment.

Nirasawa looked terrible, the right side of his face clawed to ribbons. The right eye had drooled out of its socket, lying across the ruptured mass of his cheek in a seeping, oozing bath of creamy lubricant. The white liquid had almost completely covered the front of his suit, and part of Briggs's. He looked at Lara with his good eye and she saw that his unhappiness was real, or as real as his synthesized emotional makeup would allow.

"Please, you must help Mr. Briggs," he gurgled.

Lara sighed, a little surprised at her feeling of pity for the bodyguard, although she supposed she knew where it came from. It wasn't *his* fault that he'd been created to protect assholes like Briggs; it was probably his primary function, and with Briggs as good as dead, Nirasawa was now obsolete.

"Couldn't happen to a nicer guy," Jess muttered, stepping forward to join them. Noguchi stood watch, scanning the trees, Max as still as a statue. Lara hoped he was resting, or at least not in any pain.

"When I tried to pull it off of him, he started to choke," Nirasawa said. "I'm afraid that part of my contingency awareness has been damaged. I don't know what to do."

Jess leaned down, reaching out to tap at the shell of the embryo carrier. It wobbled, and Lara saw its tail slide from around Briggs's neck, loosening. Jess put his burner down and grabbed two of its multijointed legs with each hand, the face-hugger coming away easily. A thin fluid dribbled out of Briggs's slack mouth; still unconscious, he moaned, turning his head as Jess dropped the dead carrier into the grass.

"Too late," Lara said, unable to muster any sympathy for the executive. Jess was right—if anyone deserved such a death, it was Lucas Briggs.

Nirasawa blinked, his unsocketed eye twitching on his face with a tiny wet smacking noise. "It is my job to protect him."

Even Jess seemed to feel bad for the synthetic. "Look, your boss is beyond help," he said. "He's been implanted with a parasitic embryo that will kill him. There's nothing that anyone can do, and probably nothing you could have done to stop it. You'll have to—"

"*Quiet*," Noguchi whispered, and Lara tensed, pulling her nine-millimeter, glancing back to see that Ellis had both of Max's arms raised again. Jess scooped up his burner and stepped closer to Lara.

Silence for a moment—and then there was the faintest sound of movement in the trees ahead of them, a sound like some stealthy creature might make, sliding through the dark. Lara saw a branch move, then another, meters away, but couldn't see what was making them rustle.

Noguchi took off her mask and dropped it, speaking softly, her shoulders set, her gaze unwavering.

"We're splitting up," she said, and Lara knew from the sound of her voice that this time, there wasn't going to be any discussion.

Five Hunters stepped out from the cover of the jungle, cloaked, armed only with blades. When Noguchi saw who was with them, she understood, not for the first time, that there were some fates that couldn't be avoided. Shouldn't be.

"We're splitting up," Noguchi said, dropping her burner next to her mask. If they'd been armed with heavier weapons, she probably would have passed—but as it was, the situation felt too much like an opportunity, the circumstances too perfect for coincidence.

There was a Blooded she didn't know, three novices—and Shorty. When they saw her throw her weapon down, Shorty clattered to his Leader, Noguchi too far away to hear the exchange, but knowing what it was about all the same.

Challenge. Honor.

Ellis would see Jess and Lara to the ship, they'd be fine . . . except there was the problem of the rest of the Hunters. Noguchi felt a twinge of doubt, evaluating

the group. They'd let her fight Shorty, but would kill
her when it was over, assuming she survived. Hunters
loved an honor match, but they wouldn't let her walk
away afterward.

Unless . . .

"Nirasawa," she said, still watching the Hunters,
watching as another novice took Shorty's blade from
him, "it's too late for you to help your master . . . but
if there's any part of your programming that under-
stands revenge, now's the time to access it. These are
the beings responsible for his condition."

The Hunters uncloaked, stepping farther away
from the backdrop of jungle. Shorty took off his mask,
throwing it aside, and the Hunters began to trill to one
another, clicking and clattering excitedly.

"I understand," Nirasawa said, and Noguchi
glanced back to see that he'd put his master down, laying him gently in the grass.

"The rest of you, get to the ship," Noguchi said.
"I'll be there as soon as I can."

"Machiko . . ." Lara started, but Noguchi shook
her head. There wasn't anything that she or Jess could
say that would change her mind.

"I have unfinished business here," she said grimly,
and started across the clearing, Nirasawa falling in behind her. Perhaps it was lunacy, perhaps she would
only get herself killed, fighting for an integrity that
wasn't even in question—but perhaps, after all this
time, she'd finally grasped the Hunter's way.

*It's about doing what you have to do, regardless of the
outcome. And it's about killing your enemy, because he
doesn't understand how only the strong have a right to
honor.*

With a scream of undisguised glee, Shorty stepped
out to meet her.

Ellis understood enough of what was happening to
know that Max shouldn't kill the creatures—

—badguys five object—

—so they watched without acting, as the small woman and the inorganic moved away, each step adding to the numbers that ran across Ellis's eyes, distance and speed. Ellis thought that he might be bleeding; Max didn't register a change in fluids, but there was enough wrong with Max that Ellis decided to abstain from deciding.

we have to go now, ellis, can you hear
ellis, can you
help me pick him up

Max looked down at their friends, not sure who had spoken, Ellis pleased by the sounds of their voices.

what are you doing, you said yourself that briggs is beyond help

i'll explain later ellis, help me

Jess. Jess wanted their help. He had crouched next to the unmoving human, touching him, trying to move him. Ellis explained to Max what Jess wanted and Max took a step forward, knees bending, the glowing plain of the ground line rising in front of their eyes. Ellis felt his body moving within, leaning over, and felt warmth against skin, wet motion across his lips.

Bleeding, I am bleeding.

Jess pushed the human into the crook of Max's right arm and they stood up, 82.72 kilos heavier than before. Max made adjustments for the difference, taking up enough calculation space that Ellis couldn't make out any more words.

Both humans, *Lara, Jess*, made sounds, speaking, and Ellis understood the meaning if not what they said; it was time to go.

Max and Ellis stepped forward, avoiding the distraction that was taking place nine meters away, between the small woman and the nonhuman badguys. From the sharp sounds and quick movements, they decided it was highly probable that the interaction was violent.

Ellis was glad to be leaving; he was getting tired, and thought that he might like to sleep soon.

27

Nirasawa's capacity for retaliatory action was well mapped and undamaged, a self-contained 3 LCerabyte module that had been integrated into his reasoning after his assignment to Mr. Briggs. The humans that he'd recognized, Katherine Lara and Martin Jess, had been telling the truth, as had the woman Lara had called "Machiko." No pupil dilation, no change in respiration; Mr. Briggs would not survive.

Protecting Mr. Briggs was no longer his primary function, which meant that he had to report back to his Weyland/Yutani AI Assignment Officer as soon as he could find a transmitter—and he now had the option to physically incapacitate the perpetrators of Mr. Briggs's inevitable death. The woman Machiko started for the group of five alien/organics and Nirasawa followed, the stimuli from the tapped module flooding his driver.

"Nirasawa, the small one and I will engage," Machiko said as she walked, and flexed her right arm. A pair of sharpened knives projected from the back of her wrist with a click, snapping into place. "The others may wish to involve themselves in our fight. If you choose to keep them from interfering, you will cause them psychological damage.''

Nirasawa didn't respond, but decided that inflicting more than just physical injury was appealing. His module had been designed so that associates of a damaged or dead consumer could feel that some justice had been served; it did not recommend any one method of reciprocity over any other, but did suggest that a combination of methods was highly effective.

The members of the alien group were agitated, calling out in a language Nirasawa did not know, making threatening gestures as he and Machiko neared. From his previous interaction on the Bunda station platform, Nirasawa knew that they were physically much stronger than humans, but didn't think it necessary to tell the woman; he deduced it likely that she already knew. Machiko moved ahead of him, stopping two meters from the smallest of the screaming alien beings and striking a fighting pose.

The short alien screamed again, leaping forward. When the woman dodged to avoid his attack, one of the watching creatures swiped at her with the same kind of apparatus that she wore, two pointed blades at the back of his clawed fist.

Nirasawa moved. As Machiko darted away from the second assailant, he reached forward and grabbed its shoulder, jerking it off-balance. A third alien lunged for Nirasawa with a bladed staff, damaging the silicone colloid that served as his tricep. Nirasawa still had a grip on the second attacker's shoulder. He broke it, then turned his attention to the blade carrier, aware that all four beings had now surrounded him. The woman would have her engagement with the small one.

Nirasawa was satisfied that the module was in full working order.

Noguchi saw that another novice was preparing to attack even as Shorty leapt for her. It was a feint, a classic, the second Hunter ready to skewer her as she blocked Shorty's wild lunge, designed only to intimidate her into dodging.

Pathetic.

She went with it, feinting her own dodge right, ducking well beneath the untrained swipe of Shorty's second and shifting her weight back to the left. She came up with her wrist blades, the tips of them catching the plate armor at Shorty's groin.

Shorty wheeled backwards, tusks going wide, although the blades didn't pierce flesh. Noguchi followed through, not willing to overbalance, pulling herself back up into a defensive crouch.

The screams of the others told her that Nirasawa was busy, but she didn't look away from Shorty, fully aware that one of them wouldn't be walking away from this one. Shorty knew it, too, she could see it in the shine of his hateful gaze, in the way it flickered toward his backup.

They're busy, you blustering crab. You're all mine.

"Come and get it," she sneered, grinning tightly. "*Pauk-de 'aseigan!*"

She'd either called him a fucking servant or a servant fucker, she wasn't sure. All that mattered was that it had the desired effect, goading him to reckless action.

Screaming with raw fury, Shorty jumped, swiping his blades down in an arc, all of his powerful bulk behind the violent move—

—and Noguchi dropped, one hand behind her, supporting her weight as she delivered a solid kick to his shin. Shorty rocked with the blow, using it, continuing his downward swipe as he fell—

—and Noguchi rolled to the side, Shorty's blades missing her head by centimeters. With his weight behind them, the shining knives were buried in the ground, Shorty on his side, facing her as he struggled to pull them free.

Now!

Noguchi lashed out with her right hand, so concentrated on the killing strike, already seeing the metal dripping with green from his slashed throat—

—that she didn't see his knee coming up until it made contact, slamming into the front of her left thigh hard enough to send shock pulses of agony through her body.

Noguchi was shoved back, too far for her knives to reach his spotted throat. She stumbled to her feet, favoring her injury as Shorty managed to free his wrist and get up.

She stood in defense, ready for his next lunge—but he mirrored her action. Warily, they watched each other, gazes locked, the screams of pain and fury from the other Hunters distant and unimportant.

Kill them all, android. Let this stay between us.

The eyes would give it away, she'd see him look before he leapt—but it seemed that Shorty had finally learned not to go running into a fight with his betters. Neither moved, both waiting for the opening that would end it, once and for all.

Lara and Jess stayed close to Max, Ellis seeming to understand that they wanted to head west, keeping to a reasonably straight line. They were able to move faster than before, Max tearing a path through the abundant growth, the smell of sap and cut plants surrounding them as the sound of Noguchi's battle fell behind.

Briggs's body was folded over the elbow joint of Max's right arm, Ellis keeping the arm stable as he moved so that the impregnated Briggs wouldn't fall off. The exec's arms and legs were slapped at by weeds and broken tree limbs, which was fine by Jess; Briggs's comfort wasn't high on his list of needs. Besides, he was unconscious. They probably wouldn't be able to use him at all, but Jess thought that having a still-breathing suit in tow might turn out to be extremely handy.

He won't give birth for another couple hours, at least, plenty of time in case—

"Jess, listen," Lara said, and stopped, tilting her head, her face pale as milk. Ellis took one more crashing step and did the same, turning statue.

Jess listened. He heard jungle sounds, night sounds—the *rhee-rhee-rhee* of some cicada relative, a wind in the treetops high above, the scuttling rasps underfoot of animals too small to move the leaves. They held in place for a full minute, and Jess didn't hear anything unexpected.

"I heard something moving," Lara said, chewing at her lower lip. "I'm sure."

If Lara was sure, than there was something to it. Jess moved closer to Ellis, searching the shadow-flecked trees for darker things.

"Ellis, do you see anything?"

Ellis didn't respond. Jess shot a glance at Lara, saw the same worry on her face. The kid hadn't spoken since alerting them to Nirasawa's approach; he seemed to comprehend what they wanted, but that he wouldn't talk, even to answer them, was unnerving.

What's going on in there, Ellis?

Max looked dead. Each time it stopped walking, Jess had to wonder if it would start again, the giant body turning into an object that seemed incapable of life.

"I guess—" Lara started, and then Ellis was moving.

It happened fast, Max's left arm swiveling back and up, directed into the dark and broken trail behind them. There was a *puh* of sound, of displaced air, *grenade*—

—and a sharp pop, and a dazzling light. The electric glow of white phosphorous hissed up from the burning filler some fifteen meters back, a tremendous billow of smoke pluming into the air from the M60—

—and before Jess could feel more than a second's confusion, he saw the silhouettes in front of the rising sheet of white, and heard the screech of the one that was dancing through the flame. He saw two others, standing sharply outlined by the sizzling light. Hunters.

There was the ripping sound of a burner, barely audible over the dying screams of the Hunter on fire—

—and the blast hit Max in the back, and then Jess and Lara were both firing, the burner jumping in Jess's hands, the crack of Lara's semi blending into the harsh rattle from Max's pulse rifle.

Brrrp-BOOM, the flash from Jess's burner slammed into the chest of one of them, throwing it backwards into the rising incendiary flame. There was a clattering howl, terrible, and Jess brought the weapon around to the second—

—and its body was jumping, convulsing with the hammer of bullets that pounded it all the way down, Lara and Max both shooting, its muscular form crashing to the ground.

Max ceased firing. Jess and Lara both stopped, scanning for further movement—and all was quiet, only the hiss of the white-turning-orange flames as they ate slowly through the surrounding brush. If there were any more Hunters in the area, they'd decided not to join the fight; it was over, at least for the moment.

"Unh," Max whispered, and Jess felt his heart pounding in delayed reaction, felt renewed fear for the kid as he and Lara both turned to inspect the damage.

The black, smoking splotch on Max's back was too hot to touch; Lara ripped a strip of cloth from the bottom of her shirt and balled it up, wiping it across the wide and ragged mark. The hit didn't seem to have penetrated the armor, but it had eaten through the protective acid-and heat-resist coating, *he could be boiling alive in there*—

"Ellis! Brian, are you hurt? Can you talk?" Lara asked, her voice right on the edge of panic.

Nothing—except a soft, unconscious groan from Briggs, still draped over Max's flamethrower arm. Amazingly, he hadn't been injured.

"Kid, *please*," Jess said, aching inside as well as out. "Say you're all right, say *anything*."

"Any, thing," Max breathed, and Lara laughed, the sharp sound close to a sob. Jess swallowed, hard—and faced front again, wanting this endless, painful night to be over with.

"Go, let's go," he said, taking a step forward, then two—and then Max raised one massive metal leg and put it back down, following, and Lara joined them.

Almost over, almost, Jess thought, and was still working to believe that a half klick later when they heard the trumpeting calls of at least a dozen approaching drones.

28

Three of the four beings were dead or disabled, but Nirasawa had suffered considerable damage in the effort. Seven major latchment points between musculature and skeleton had been severed through his back and left side, seriously incapacitating the feedback systems that kept him stable. Overall electrical stim received for his limb colloids was down 37 percent—and the casing for his hydrogen fuel cell had been pierced, which, if further damaged, would very likely relieve him of all processing capability. He would become inert; he would cease.

Studying the stance of the last viable opponent, Nirasawa could see that the being's injuries were also significant. From the labored breathing to the unreliability and tissue damage of its right leg, Nirasawa thought that it would die soon without medical attention. Still, it continued to present itself as an opponent, and Nirasawa meant to alter its status. The woman had not finished her engagement with the being she fought, and Nirasawa wanted to aid her in destroying the last of Mr. Briggs's killers.

The ailing creature stepped forward, jabbing its staff at Nirasawa. Nirasawa pushed the blade aside, moving in, bringing his right arm up and delivering a blow to the alien's probable ribs. Several snapped.

The creature clattered loudly in its own language, a pale green blood washing from its mouth—and its damaged leg crumpled. The being fell, gasping, and Nirasawa bent down, reaching for its throat—

—and the creature, with some final burst of strength, thrust its staff deep into Nirasawa's abdomen.

The fuel cell itself was punctured. Nirasawa felt the energy shut down, first to his legs. He collapsed on top of the gasping creature, driving his right elbow into its neck, hearing the wet collapse of its airway.

Nirasawa's arms went next. Then the pump of lubricant faltered, the stability and latchment systems releasing a short and final jolt of stim through his immobile limbs. He could no longer move.

Nirasawa's one functioning eye saw the stars in the Bunda sky, and then that, too, ceased to operate. There was a flush of nonsequential numbers in the dark—and then Nirasawa was no more.

Noguchi heard the dying call of the Blooded Hunter, a trilled greeting to the Black Warrior, a final shuffle of movement—and then nothing. Nirasawa had fallen, and the other Hunters were dead.

Just you and me now.

Shorty had managed one glancing blow to her side, and she had raked his right arm with the blades, but neither had gained the advantage. They continued their circling appraisal of one another, Noguchi knowing that Shorty wouldn't be able to hold out for much longer. He was yautja, and young; she'd seen Blooded maintain a defense, but Shorty would eventually feel that he was cowardly for not attacking. She was betting on it.

And if you're wrong? This could go on, and other Hunters will come, and your victory will mean nothing . . .

Noguchi felt the seconds tick by like minutes, her every muscle tensed, watchful for his next move. He hadn't responded to further taunting; she'd called him small and weak, she'd stumbled through a few proverbs about having no honor. If she could just find something that would reignite his fury, push him into another reckless act . . .

Think! The names he'd called her in the past, the things he'd said in the hope of hurting her. Woman, human, alien—nothing there, nothing that had come across as more than a mild slight.

Except—he thought they were horrible slurs. The very worst he could come up with . . .

She had it. Noguchi knew what to say. She ran through the words in her head, preparing herself for his assault as she decided on her counterstrike.

"*Chi'-dte ooman-di,*" Noguchi said. "*Lou'-dte Dahdtoudi kalei!*"

Shorty flew at her as the last word left her mouth, his face shocked and sick with rage, his blades swinging wildly.

Noguchi was already in motion, leaping away from the pitiful strike, jumping—

—and landing a solid kick to the side of his right knee, where she'd kicked him in their match on the *Shell,* where he should still be hurting. Shorty howled, falling to the ground, instantly pushing himself off and coming for her—

—and she slashed, the diamond-sharp wrist blades melting through his forearm. Blood spouted up as his right hand folded, hanging from cut bone and sliced flesh by the wet sinewy tendons, the only thing still connecting his claws to his arm.

Shorty screamed again, in agony, grabbing at the pounding flow from his wrist and stumbling at her. Unable to comprehend that he'd lost.

"You're not Hunter!" Noguchi shouted as she side-stepped his clumsy attempt, not caring if he understood. "*I* am, and I'm better at it than any of you arrogant, bullying *children*!"

Shorty crashed into the dirt, still hugging his useless arm, trilling in pain and denial. Noguchi stood over him, feeling the beat of her human heart, realizing how much time she'd wasted caring about what the Hunters believed—and understanding that she was free from them, that her human spirit had conquered.

With the help of a few carefully chosen words . . .

She'd told Shorty that he loved human women, and that he obviously wanted to father her children. How wonderful, that it was his own conceit and intolerance that had cost him the battle. How typical.

How very *yautja*.

Noguchi stared down at the suffering Hunter for a moment longer, then knelt by him, staring into his spiteful, hurting face.

"*Human*," he spat, and Noguchi nodded, not at all surprised that he could speak the word clearly.

"That's right," she said, and plunged her wrist blades into his throat. She watched his eyes, watched the spark of life leaving him, feeling only triumph.

A moment later, he was dead. Noguchi stood up, flicking the hot blood from her blades and retracting them, looking around at the body-littered clearing. Nirasawa was gone, ruined, but he'd managed to take out four Hunters first. Three had been unBlooded, but the fourth had surely been a challenge, the etched star shape on his brow marking him warrior.

Noguchi reached up and touched her own mark, thinking of Broken Tusk, wondering if he would have approved the things she'd done. She was still proud to wear his symbol, and thought that he would have understood—but it occurred to her that it didn't particularly matter whether or not he would have supported her actions. He wasn't there—and as trite as it seemed, she knew that it was her opinion and hers only that mattered. It had always been that way, but she'd forgotten for a while.

Noguchi turned away, looking for her burner. She had a ship to catch.

Lara heard the bugs coming through the jungle and her heart sank. So close, they had to be less than half a kilometer from the Hunter transport, and she simply didn't know how much longer she could go on. Max was faltering, his steps slowing, and Jess had tripped and fallen twice since their encounter with the Hunters. They'd been through so much, the space station, Briggs, facing death again and again through all of it—

—and Jess is about to collapse, and Ellis could very well die any moment, and I'm so, so tired—

Lara gritted her teeth, forcing the thoughts away. They *were* close, and she'd faced bugs before. It was still very dark—although it had to be early morning by now—but drones made more than enough noise to target. She was down to her last few rounds, but she was a good shot, she knew she could make them count.

Ellis may not be able to help, but Jess will hang on . . . Whether or not he could aim very well anymore wasn't something she wanted to consider, but she stepped closer to him, both of them standing close to Max. If he couldn't do it, she'd take the burner when she ran out of bullets.

They were getting closer, at least ten, fifteen of them, the sounds of their approach violent and wild, trees snapping, their chittering shrieks growing louder.

"Ten o'clock," Jess said, and Lara nodded—

—and then Ellis spoke, his shaky voice quiet and small.

"Stay back we kill," he said, and Max's arms both locked forward, Briggs's body sliding to the ground in a heap.

Before Lara could consider the implications of "we," the first drone tore into the open, ten meters

away. And Max took one step forward and became
death, the world catching fire at his touch.

Maxellis saw the first break cover and opened up, no
longer certain of the best kill method, no longer able to
mark an exact distance. They fired everything, deciding
in waves of red-and-black awareness that a solid curtain of defense would probably work.

Flame erupted from Maxellis's right hand, a stream
of napthal that stretched to meet the XT, its bounding
form halting, screaming, turning in circles as its fluids
heated and expanded. Its exoskeleton burst, and Maxellis were already working the next moving forms,
finding them, sending HEAP and incendiary grenades
into the midst of the tumbling bodies.

—we kill and thirteen more—

Part of Maxellis had been injured by heat, when
there had still been a separation. The fusion had been
necessary for the good of the whole, although elements
of both halves had been lost. There was no pain, but
very little clarity, either, the entity's self-awareness
muddled, incomplete.

Maxellis did not think of this as they sent two full
cartridges of rounds into the jungle, two hundred
armor-piercers that tore through legs and arms, mists
of drone blood flying, exo shrapnel from the exploding
bodies slamming into other bodies. The napthal continued to stream across the congregation, burning to
death those that didn't fall right away.

In less than two minutes, it was over. The only
movement in the burning was the burning itself,
smoke and flame rising and twisting up, finding new
things to burn.

The Lara and Jess were speaking, but Maxellis's capacity for speech was extremely limited, their understanding of language reduced to fundamentals.

We go now assigned parcel—

The body. Maxellis turned and picked it up, doing

as little damage as they could to the fragile flesh. Then they turned and moved ahead, in the direction that they had been going since before the meld.

In a matter of moments, they had reached the destination.

29

Noguchi ran through the dark, aware that time was short. She'd heard the explosions only minutes after leaving her battlefield, and knew that the Hunters would head for the sight and sound of action. It was surely that suit, Max, and she hoped that the firefight meant Lara and Jess were still alive, that Ellis was protecting them.

The trees whipped past, Noguchi concentrating on keeping balanced, on skirting obstacles and keeping her speed up. She didn't want to be left behind; her fight on Bunda was over, and she was more than ready to be away from the Hunt.

And the Hunters, who wouldn't mind at all if I missed my flight.

Noguchi picked up speed, moving faster.

The Hunter transport was twice as big as the *Nemesis* shuttle, and looked something like a water pitcher lying on its side, a rounded body tapering at the neck. Jess wouldn't particularly care if it looked like a giant dog turd; he'd never been so happy to see anything.

The ship had set down in an angled clearing, near the top of a gently sloping hill, the jungle they stepped out of at the bottom. The sky seemed lighter, perhaps because of the open space, or maybe because the endless night was actually ending; they moved into the pale light away from the trees, Jess grateful to get out of the secretive dark.

At least we'll see the next deadly thing coming . . . He considered crossing his fingers but thought it might be his undoing, the final exertion that would knock him out cold. He wouldn't be good for much longer.

Together, he and Lara struggled to keep up with the Max as it marched easily to the ship, holding Briggs with both arms. Throughout all of it, Briggs still hadn't come out of his postimplant coma. Jess knew that they'd have to leave the exec behind; he'd thought that they could use him if they ran into any Company people, but—

"I'll see about the controls," Lara gasped, breaking into his wandering thoughts as they neared the vehicle. "You get Ellis out of that thing."

Jess nodded, suddenly feeling more vulnerable than he had in the wooded jungle. He was afraid of what he would find when he opened the suit. Ellis had referred to himself and the Max as "we" before blowing up the band of drones that had come for them, and he'd been an emotional mess already, ever since 949. Jess had been with him for the first interface, and remembered how he'd gradually declined, losing his speech, becoming erratic—losing *himself*. . . .

. . . *we'll take care of you, kid. Don't die on us—and don't stop being Ellis.*

That was the worst of his fears, he knew, even worse than that Ellis might die from the second interface. The thought that Ellis might not be there anymore, that the spark of his character might be gone—

—*no. He'll be fine, everything will be fine.* Jess held on to the thought, determined to believe it.

They reached the ship, and it looked even more

alien up close. It was made from some light gray material, matte and smooth, not a straight line in sight. Even the hatch was rounded, a giant stretched oval set into the side of the swollen body. Lara reached up and touched a panel next to the door, Jess holding his breath—and exhaling as the hatch slid to one side with a soft hum.

Inside, it looked more like a transport shuttle, with obvious chairs and a rounded console at the front. It was spacious and empty, and smelled faintly of something sour.

Lara moved inside, and Jess turned to Max, standing a few meters away. Even Hunter-sized, the door was too small to admit the bulky suit; he'd have to pull Ellis out and carry him into the ship.

"Okay, Ellis. Breathe easy, I'm going to—"

Max raised his rifle arm, pointing it down the hill, cutting Jess short, making him feel sick. Something was coming. It was as if every pain in Jess's body surfaced at once, the full extent of his injury and exhaustion finally letting itself be known.

No more. God, no more.

Jess turned, aching—

—and saw Machiko Noguchi emerge from the tangle of trees.

Maxellis was safe and warm in the dark, feeling nothing, aware that the smallwoman was not a threat. They kept the left arm raised anyway, in case she was not alone.

She moved quickly up the grade and spoke to the Jess, the man, both of them making soft and light sounds, good sounds. She stood and waited for something, her posture expectant.

The man moved behind Maxellis and touched the damaged area of their body. They realized too late what he was doing and tried to tell him no, no, that it was not good—

—and there was a shock of sensation, of many, ice

and wet and pain. Maxellis screamed soundlessly, born into the terrible cold, pulled from their womb of sustenance—

—and then there was nothing.

Lara sat in the center of the circular console, confused, not sure what to touch to make the alien ship come to life. She'd *found* the controls, at least—there were a dozen flat squares that might be buttons facing the blank front viewscreen, with two thick handles sitting above them. She'd punched the first square in the line and it had lit up, a deep red color. As far as she could tell, that was all it had done.

Intuitive, right . . .

She was about to try the next when she heard Noguchi's voice coming from the open hatch behind her.

"I can pilot, come help—"

Lara stood and turned, hugely relieved at the sound of the woman's firm voice—until she saw Ellis in Noguchi's arms, streaks of drying blood on his ashen face. His hair was matted with red.

"Oh, shit," Lara said weakly, and hurried out from behind the controls, stumbling to where Noguchi stood. Together, they moved Ellis to one of the benches against the wall, laying him down as gently as possible.

Noguchi moved to the controls and slid into the pilot seat, running her hand across the buttons from left to right. Immediately, the ship began to rumble, a steady sound of working machinery filling the faintly unpleasant air. At the same time, the front viewscreen flickered on, and Lara glanced up at it from where she'd collapsed, cradling Ellis's poor head in her lap.

The picture was surprisingly sharp, the colors muted, the view of the hill's base where the clearing met the jungle. Lara started to look away, to look for a supply cabinet, *they have to have bandages of some kind*—

—when she saw the darkness coil out into the open space.

"*Jess!*" Lara screamed, staring at the dozens of bugs

that were surging out of the trees, at the running black tide of teeth and claws erupting into the clearing.

"He said he was—" Noguchi started, but then Jess was falling inside, tripping across the smooth floor to where Lara sat, landing in the seat next to her.

"Go, go, I'm in!" Jess shouted.

"Hang on, we're—"

Bam bam bam bam!

Noguchi whipped around, staring at the still-open hatch. "Who's shooting?"

"Briggs, I put him in Max," Jess said. "Now go!"

The drones were coming, the dark wave drawing closer, and over the sound of a pulse rifle Lara could hear their rising screams—and could see the front line crumbling, the closest of the trumpeting animals blown back by the steady beat of Max's firing—

—and then the hatch was closed, and Lara held on to Ellis as the transport jerked and lifted, rising up from in front of the teeming mass, from the sudden river of liquid fire that swept across the dark, insectile bodies.

Flamethrower.

Lara turned wide eyes to Jess, still not sure that she'd heard right.

"You put Briggs—"

Jess reached down and touched Ellis's forehead, brushing the hair away from his waxy brow. "Thought he could do some good with the time he has left," Jess muttered.

The transport rose for another few seconds and then shot away.

30

Lara and Jess had done what they could for their friend, bandaging him with a few pieces of soft leather they'd found for cleaning weapons. There was a medkit on board, but the tough plastic patches that Hunters used as bandages weren't made for humans, and Noguchi didn't know about any of the shots or drug packs.

There was plenty of air, enough for at least two weeks, and ancient emergency rations that had been stocked on the slight chance that something went wrong on a Hunt, stranding the Hunters. The protein jerky would taste terrible, she knew from experience, but it would sustain them.

As the transport began its ascent into Bunda's outer atmosphere, Lara and Jess moved forward, taking seats near the piloting console. Noguchi glanced back and saw that they'd strapped the unconscious Ellis to a bench, his arms folded across his narrow chest. It was amazing to her, how young he was. She'd pictured him as much older, as a lined and weathered man, but the person Jess had pulled out of the suit barely looked out of his teens. With his face wiped clean, he seemed even more like a child, pale and fragile.

"How is he?" Noguchi asked.

Lara answered. "His pulse is good, but beyond that . . ."

She trailed off, and the three of them sat quietly for a moment. Noguchi could hardly believe that it was over; not just their experience on Bunda, but her life with the Clan.

"So, where do we go from here?" Jess asked softly, his eyes closed, his voice thick with approaching sleep.

"Home," Lara said, looking out at the approaching stars, her expression peaceful, tired, and a little sad but at rest.

Home.

Lara was talking about Earth, but Noguchi thought there was more to it, the planet's name inspiring none of the warm and lovely things that Lara's answer had inspired. It was the word for feelings she'd never fully understood and she savored it, tasting it, wondering how it could mean so much now.

Home. Someplace I haven't been, yet.

They moved out into the void, the soothing lull of the engines putting her passengers to sleep, Noguchi looking forward to experiences she knew would put the Hunt to shame, to a life that would be whole and fulfilling and new; they were going home.

EPILOGUE

He slept, and as he had before, he dreamed.

He dreamed in concepts, in pictures of ideas. That there was strength and heat in the cold emptiness, that there was light in the dark, that time and thought were fluid, yielding to the pressure of his touch. He dreamed that there was no loneliness, no pain—and when the fabric of his dreams began to thin, when shredded, ugly holes began to appear in the fine cloth, he fought bitterly to keep his dreams close to him, to keep himself whole.

It was no use. After what seemed an eternal struggle the beautiful darkness melted away, and there was pain, and he was alone. The war was lost . . . but he thought that his name was Brian, and in thinking it, felt that perhaps losing wasn't the end of everything good.

He settled into a deep and healing sleep, and did not dream anymore.

ABOUT THE AUTHOR

S. D. (STEPHANI DANELLE) PERRY writes multimedia novelizations in the fantasy/science fiction/horror genres for love and money. Besides several works in the *Aliens* universe, she has adapted the scripts for *Timecop* and *Virus* and written a *Xena, Warrior Princess* novel under the name Stella Howard. She also writes books based on video-games.

S. D. and her husband live in Portland, Oregon, with two sweet dogs and a rather nasty hedgehog named Miles.